THE CURRICULUM VITAE
OF AURORA ORTIZ

Almudena Solana

THE CURRICULUM VITAE
OF AURORA ORTIZ

Translated from the Spanish by
David Frye

THE HARVILL PRESS
LONDON

Published by The Harvill Press, 2005

2 4 6 8 10 9 7 5 3 1

© Almudena Solana, 2002, 2005
English translation © David Frye, 2005

Almudena Solana has asserted her right under the Copyright, Designs
and Patents Act 1988 to be identified as the author of this work

First published with the title *El currículum de Aurora Ortiz*
by Editorial Punto de Lectura, S.A., 2002

First published in Great Britain in 2005 by
The Harvill Press
Random House
20 Vauxhall Bridge Road
London SW1V 2SA

Random House Australia (Pty) Limited
20 Alfred Street, Milsons Point, Sydney,
New South Wales 2061, Australia

Random House New Zealand Limited
18 Poland Road, Glenfield,
Auckland 10, New Zealand

Random House South Africa (Pty) Limited
Endulini, 5A Jubilee Road, Parktown 2193, South Africa

The Random House Group Limited Reg. No. 954009
www.randomhouse.co.uk

A CIP catalogue record for this book is available from the British Library

ISBN 1 84343 0967

Papers used by Random House are natural,
recyclable products made from wood grown in sustainable forests;
the manufacturing processes conform to the environmental
regulations of the country of origin

Typeset by Palimpsest Book Production Limited,
Polmont, Stirlingshire

Printed and bound in Great Britain by
William Clowes Ltd, Beccles, Suffolk

To my mother. To my father.

*To all those who work in whatever way they
can and who, in spite of it all,
enjoy doing their job well.*

"The real idlers are these: the ones who say they are working, but who do nothing but let themselves be stunned into stifling their thoughts"

MIGUEL DE UNAMUNO
Niebla

CHAPTER I

Yes, I want a job. I would take any job. But if it were possible, I'd like to choose: I'd prefer to be the caretaker of a peaceful building; one of those buildings that have a little caretaker's office, with a chair behind a desk. I know times are hard, but I can send references. Above all, I recognise my own limitations, so I won't skimp on my story – I wouldn't want you to say I didn't warn you.

My birth took an unusually long time. I was probably distracted by the bubbles that gurgled around me as I was developing my ears, which brought sounds to me from far away; or else I was noticing, with dazed wonder, that I had five fingers on each hand. I spent ten months, not comprehending what was going on, until a sudden sneeze finally brought me out somewhere in the world. All right, somewhere in Galicia. In the North-west of Spain. I'll describe it that way to keep things general, because I doubt you'd know exactly where my village is, and knowing its name won't tell you anything more about it.

After I was born, they started singing me the song about the she-wolf and her five little cubs. I looked again at my hands with their five little fingers, but I couldn't see the connection. I was just as surprised to discover my feet, and other people's feet, and other people's faces. And my mother's hugs. (I don't know why I'm telling you all this, but allow me to continue.)

When my little world began to seem too small, I began to fill it out with the names for people and personalities, arms and legs, and more: rivers, tributaries, and other accidents of geography. I found something to surprise myself with every day, and I filed each new bit of data away in the most immaculate order, diligently listing it all in coloured felt tip pens. Then the years passed by; so many years that they decided I was ready for the advanced courses, where students spoke easily about Socrates and Plato. The blackboard filled up with long Latin phrases, and a few words even showed off their Greek letters.

But even after all that education, everything I had learned during so many years of enthusiastic listening could have been written down in just one of those big spiral notebooks; and, of course, if you tried to make me talk about it today, I couldn't guarantee that it would come out in any kind of order. I'd mix up all the times and places, confuse the riots and mayhem of history with the organised uprisings. Though in reality I would still be able to tell the heart of the matter from the froth. That ability, and an impudent self-confidence, will see me through.

So here you have me. Wanting to be a caretaker for a building.

I told you straight off that I was even lazy about being born, 30 years ago; but for some reason, today I feel lucky that I've been lost in daydreams ever since I was little. I've become so disillusioned by forgetting everything that seemed utterly crucial to me when I was studying it, that I'm thrilled now to think that my efforts weren't entirely useless after all, and that the impression those facts leave on a person are truly interesting. Now all my studies and all my awards seem less high-flying, and I can give them the importance that they truly deserve – which is to say, very little.

I am offering to spend my working days sitting behind the desk in a caretaker's office. I know that, from there, I can travel far. As you can see, I haven't described an interest in any particular field of study; however, if you were to ask me, I could write you a whole treatise on what being and nothingness mean to my cousin Anselmo, who teaches philosophy in a private school in Santiago – he's a fine scholar, who never splits hairs. His mother, my aunt Domi, is a hairdresser, and splitting hairs is something she knows all about.

Everybody in my family has a job now; every last one of them is getting along and making a fairly decent living. Except for me. That is why I am writing this c.v., which, as you can see, isn't worth much because of the patchy way I've put my education to use. But I freely admit to you that I've made my peace with my own ignorance, because, thanks to it, I've discovered how absolutely necessary it is for me to learn.

If you gave me a caretaker's job, I could concentrate on my books again – once I had finished taking out the rubbish, of course. During the course of the day, on the other hand (since the working day is long, although that doesn't worry me), I'd listen to anybody who had something to say, because if there is one thing that motivates me, it is my terrific curiosity.

You tell me if I'm not curious. I'm telling all of you about my whole life, but all the while, what I'm really wondering is: who is there on the other side of the paper, reading everything I'm saying? A serious fellow; or perhaps a young girl; or an older woman who hasn't managed to get pregnant; or one of those "Type A" executives, but one who's feeling sad because his father is ill; or who knows . . . But in any case, I'll just say "all of you", because I'm sure these important matters have to pass through several offices. Imagine, I even feel like I should cook up a tortilla for all of you, just in case you're feeling hungry in the middle of the day and you want a taste! I've noticed that the placement office where I'm sending this letter isn't far from where I live.

I don't want to alarm you. The fact of the matter is that, as I've said, I am very curious about everything and so I've been putting down whatever comes into my head; but what I really want to get across to you is that I am very eager to learn, which I haven't been able to do up to now because of the difficulties of life and because of my parents' bad luck (well, my mother's, really). They've always led complicated lives.

I am also very eager to work.

I'll end here. I don't want to leave you with a poor impression, by which I mean you'll think I'm prone to verbal diarrhoea. No. When I'm working (if I get the job, thanks to San Pancracio and to your kind sympathy), I won't talk any more than I am required to by the owners and tenants in the building, the postman, and other professionals in that field. I certainly appreciate the fact that a peaceful caretaker's office is one that is watched over by a professional who believes in order, prudence and education. Each person in his place. And me, in my caretaker's office.

I would like to end this by thanking all of you, of course, and by thanking my neighbour who offered to help me by using her computer to write down for you everything that I have been dictating to her. The poor girl has spent the whole evening with me, and tomorrow at the break of dawn she has to go running off to one of those supermarkets that sell products at budget prices. She is going to be a checkout operator; she's starting out there, with benefits and everything. Her mother applied for her after she'd received an ad for the job in her letter box; she was the right age – unlike me, I just turned 30, but I don't care, because I'd prefer the caretaker's job. Her name is Fany, and if things don't turn out well for her, maybe I'll help her, and we'll write to you, enquiring about something for her.

NOTE: Please see the attached references. Well, if we are going to be honest with each other, I don't have any references, because I've never worked for anyone except my aunt, but please allow me to suggest that I can ask for referrals from my friends. They are all working in responsible jobs and can certainly write to you on official letterhead; I hear that an evaluation counts more that way. I feel I can say they would all tell you that I am a trustworthy girl. I hope that you will see things the same way.

Sincerely,
Aurora Ortiz

*

She had terrible doubts about every single line she had dictated to her first-floor neighbour. It was already eleven o'clock, and Aurora could no longer keep her from leaving her house, now that Fany had typed "Sincerely" and started gathering up the papers with frenetic speed. Fany assumed Aurora was happy, now they'd finished the chore that had eaten up their whole Sunday afternoon. And so it seemed: Aurora was beaming a forced smile at her, while wishing her good night.

"Thanks, Fany. It's fabulous."

But her thoughts came out in a muddle.

"Listen," she said, speaking timidly through the open door to her neighbour, who would hardly be able to help her make changes the next day. "Listen, Fany, do you think I'm the person who wrote this?"

"What do you mean?"

"Do you think I'm the person I say I am?"

"Of course, Aurora. A straight-talking girl, who comes out

and tells them she wants a job as a caretaker, and asks them if they have one for her – what could be clearer than that?"

"I don't know how these things are supposed to be done. I've never written about what I can do; and besides, it makes it harder that I've never had a job, you know."

"You're going to bowl them over. You even invited them to try your tortilla!"

"Thing is, I don't know what's happening to me, but I've been thinking so much about getting a job, about how to convince them, how to win them over to my side, or at least look all right, you know, that it's like . . . like I should at least send it in at an appropriate time. Can I tell you something? You'll think I'm crazy, but I think about them so much that it feels like I've known them my whole life."

"So why don't you give it to them in person? The agency is just around the corner."

"No! What if I show up, and they're wrapped up in their work? I wouldn't know where to start."

"Well, then, post it. That's not a bad idea, either. Everything'll be fine, you'll see," Fany said as she headed down the stairs, trying to put an end to the day and to the conversation. "And let's see how I do tomorrow. Be thinking of me," she half shouted from the lower landing.

"Sure thing, Fany. Good night. Thanks."

She read her c.v. over three more times that night before she finally dumped it in the letter box. There were things she would have changed, but she faced the problem of the computer – a subject she hadn't yet studied, and with the machine turned off, she found it even more inaccessible, unapproachable, impossible. Besides (as Aurora well knew), if she started to make changes, she wouldn't be able to keep from clipping it here and there, and who knows what would become of her life narrative and of all her neighbour's Sunday volunteer work. It was like what her Aunt Domi, the hairdresser, used to tell her; that if you want to change your hairdo, you have to do it all-out, not just by trimming your fringe without looking at your whole head of hair.

And in her heart, she knew that her c.v. was crying out for major changes.

She stood in front of the full-length mirror in her room and, as if by a reflex, stretched her arm out towards the bedside table to pick up her trimming kit. Then she trimmed the tips of her fringe with her manicure scissors. As she always did. Her hair, the colour of a suede shoe darkened by long use, still had the hues that had shone through it in her childhood; by tremendous oversimplification, people called it chestnut brown, but her Aunt Domi insisted that there were many other hues in her niece's thick mane.

Fringe trimmed above the eyes. The rest of her hair hanging to her shoulders, framing a strong, angular face: nose and chin racing to see which would reach the finish line first. Still, the overall effect was one of balance. Forehead with thick eyebrows, hidden in part by the fringe, but also a pair of honey-golden eyes that could throw light on any doubt, overcome any imperfection, and set anyone who caught sight of them dreaming.

She looked at herself straight-on when she was done. Trimming her fringe was something she had down pat. Her record was three minutes, though it made no sense to time the process; she had all the time in the world.

Now she took advantage of the full-length mirror to look herself over: up, down, behind, in profile, breathing deeply, squaring her shoulders. She was strong, and her 30-year-old body, a size 40, cut a fine figure. Good looking, and not much trouble to keep it up. Just the habit of lifting milk cartons.

She already had them. A litre and a half of skimmed in each hand. Up, down. One more time: open, close. Arms meeting in front, as if to applaud with giant hands. Fingers firmly grasping the cartons: now her elbows had to touch, in front, and behind.

Done with the arms.

Wide brown bands of rubber. Time for the leg workout. Milk cartons tied to the ankles, and then, kneeling, she lifted her right leg behind her into a right angle. Then the left. Stretch back, to the side, then the other leg . . .

She did these exercises first thing every morning after coffee, but after spending all Sunday glued to the computer with Fany, she needed to loosen up a little.

She felt comfortable in her basketball jersey. She thought again about how easy it is to express yourself in thoughts, to project yourself in moving images, without exchanging a single word. How did this power vanish?

She recalled Flaubert. "Was it Flaubert, or some other writer?" she asked herself, face down on the rug, while she raised her right leg before entering the cool of the shower. "I don't remember . . . Was he the one who wrote to a girl, telling her that the closer the words stuck to the thoughts, the better? Doesn't matter. I think I threw too many thoughts at them, and told them too little," she said in the middle of the stretch. "Maybe that worked in Flaubert's time, but it does me no good today."

Switch legs.

"But what could be more sincere than throwing my thoughts straight at them, without holding anything back?"

Switch rubber band, switch cartons.

Then she realised where the error lay.

"Fany just transcribed everything as I dictated it to her. Shouldn't she have changed it a little bit? Come on, that's why she's the writer. She could have – I don't know – made it sound more impressive, like an ad on the telly, or a personal in the papers," she said, facing the wall now and feeling a bit edgy.

"If I had them here in front of me now, the guys who are supposed to be deciding whether I get a job, I'd be eating them for breakfast, between one exercise and the next, and then we'd finish it off with a carton of milk. What a mess!" She smiled a smile of conscious defeat.

"Young woman, good reader, hard-working, desires a position as building caretaker. Flexible hours. Terms negotiable," she announced in an imposing voice.

"That's it! That's what I should have said! Or is it? Is that who I really am?"

"How ridiculous can you be, Aurora?" she angrily concluded. "You're such a bore! What difference could it possibly make whether it's me or not, if all they are going to look at is whether you can work hard, or . . . whatever! After all, you read this kind of work-wanted personal every day. But that's more the ads you see in the papers. So . . ."

She left the thought dangling.

And finished her exercises.

Aurora had always been a dynamic woman, a fine specimen, a very cheery specimen; afflicted with bad luck, but disinclined to let it get her down; an acrobat tumbling through life, a tightrope walker laughing at danger, a natural-born athlete – if only she could get paid for exercising with milk cartons and pimiento jars – one of those fighters who might lose a match but who never are defeated; a bundle of doubt wearing slippers indoors and boots on the street; a genuine traveller, though Madrid was the farthest she had ever gone; an enthusiastic, persistent women who loved a good conversation . . . She hadn't dictated any of this to Fany, because she didn't even know it about herself.

She just kept thinking about her letter.

"Curious, right . . . At least I told them, plain as day, that I have a lot of curiosity," she said out loud, and shook away her thoughts.

She turned off the kitchen taps and suddenly said, "Today, fruit diet," and so the night ended early, without supper.

Nor was there a television blaring in the background; but there was a short walk around the block, like the ones taken by people who have dogs and have to walk them at night even when they'd rather not go out. Aurora picked up her manila envelope, slapped an important-looking stamp on it, gritted her teeth, and left the flat carrying her c.v.

Just like someone dragging a dog by the leash to a tree so it'll do its business there and get it over with, Aurora dragged her c.v. to the yellow letter box and let the envelope fall into the open mouth that read "Madrid". Then she stared at the sky above her adopted city, like a dog owner waiting for a rapid evacuation of another creature's bowels.

There wasn't much action to wait for; at most, the distant closeness she felt to a certain office building that she knew well from the outside. Aurora knew that her letter was addressed to an office that stood directly in front of her, in front of the letter box. The envelope would just have to cross the street, directed by the large letters she had scrawled across the front in faded cobalt-blue ink: *Talento Temporary Recruitment Agency*.

CHAPTER II

"What time is it?" Aurora wondered as she opened the kitchen door. Up went the right sleeve on her jersey; a diminutive watch read 10 a.m. She felt the warmth of the coal stove, the best thing about the flat, and as the door swung closed she remembered what some refined gent had said about watches on a television talk show, the programme hosted by the famous Blanca Rosa; something about how, at the dawn of the new millennium, watches should be big. He had gone on to explain that fashion trends were heading toward an elegant minimalism, and that this sense of elegance dictated that it was better to wear fewer items on the wrist, but that they should be large and well-made, rather than many small, shoddy things.

All the women on the set had immediately applauded; women who were all older than Aurora (who was not even 31 yet), but who, like her, all wore coquettish little watches, tiny and feminine; and also all had permed hair and layers of necklaces around their necks.

"I don't know what anybody could find to object to about this watch, you know."

She looked at it: ten past ten in the morning.

She recalled her husband. When he had given it to her, he was handsome as could be. Truly the Robert Mitchum of the neighbourhood, and of her life.

"Here you go, Auro", Roberto had told her. "It wasn't the

nicest one in the jeweller's. I'll be buying you better ones later on."

At that moment, Aurora had wanted to smother her lifelong boyfriend, who would soon become her husband, with kisses. Two days later they were married in the church of San Antonio de la Florida, and they celebrated the wedding in grand style at Casa Mingo. The whole restaurant, just for them; between the bride's guests and the groom's, they came to nearly a hundred.

A hundred grieving people two years later, when she became a widow. She would have been happy with 50, if any of them, even half, had conveyed a little cheer or serenity, when all she was getting was anguished phone calls.

Roberto had died suddenly, two years after promising to love Aurora until death did them part, and also exactly two years after he had started working for Renfe, the national railway system, with a good chance of advancement due to the improvements being made to the North Madrid train station.

He had a heart attack right there, at the ticket window.

"What are you going to do now?" everyone asked Aurora.

"If we can be of any help, all you have to do is call . . ." But then they'd go back to the second person as soon as they had the chance; for example, when they started planting doubts in her mind about "how you're going to solve this" and "how you're going to solve that".

And solve it she did. Forget about being a widow: she preferred to go back to being his girlfriend, but 30 years old now, as if Roberto had taken a train from the North Madrid station and kept going north from there. That was three years ago. He hasn't come back, of course, and she isn't waiting for him, but this trick of the mind allows Aurora to be what she's always been, a woman who can't be changed, just the way he liked her: strong, brave, even-keeled, cheerful in spite of it all.

"Aurora, what a responsibility," he had told her when she

woke in his arms on their honeymoon. He had been lying there awake for hours, looking at her. "What a responsibility, having to care for you, my love."

"I can take care of myself, no fear. All you have to do is love me for ever."

Their embrace that day would have been the envy of anyone who had seen it. Aurora could still feel it, and all the embraces that came after.

They had truly loved each other. Even though he had gone off unexpectedly, they had left nothing unsaid, no reason to be sad. At least, that was the assumption that worked for Aurora and helped her fight her heartache – one of her "theoretical-practical" philosophies that got her out of every tight spot, as her friend Fany liked to say.

Boyfriend and girlfriend, nine years. Man and wife, two. And now, boyfriend and girlfriend for another three years already. And here she was, alone in her flat, rather alone when she left the flat, too, and no coffee in the pantry.

She took a few steps towards the wall clock at the end of the corridor, but first she picked up a key from the bedside table to open up the inner mechanism of the clock. She kept a few odd souvenirs in there, and a couple of pieces of jewellery: the pearls that her mother-in-law had given her on her wedding day, her parents' wedding bands, and her own. Also, Roberto's watch.

He had been given it one hot Saturday afternoon when they had gone to hear about the advantages of having a 20-volume set of the Universal Encyclopaedia at home, which they could purchase in 40 easy monthly payments. If you listened through to the end, you'd win a man's quartz wristwatch. And they had.

They had listened for an hour and a half to everything they would be able to learn if they bought the Encyclopaedia. In the end, they left their address and told the salesman that they'd think it over.

Good thing Roberto had ignored his wife, who kept having doubts, even though she managed to act her well-rehearsed part in this play: nod, show lots of interest, hands off the change purse.

But suddenly Aurora, a terrible actress with a big heart, began to falter. She thought about the happiness they could give to the man, who was describing in such detail the wisdom they'd receive by learning about history and the advancement of science. They were listening to a true enthusiast; more than that, a defender of the whole new order of life, a real architect of the future, who was preaching to an audience of four people with as much verve as if the pavilion were brimming full. Nothing would make you suspect that he had told the same story seven times before that day, and that he had three more hours to go.

"How can anybody be so enthusiastic at four in the afternoon?" Roberto wondered, with a look of studied interest, and his gaze fixed forward.

"The era of competition is over!" the employee of the well-known publishing house proclaimed. "The age of competition has been succeeded by the age of the connoisseur! This is a quiet revolution. How many times have we heard the term 'quality of life'?"

"How many times?" he repeated his question.

"Lots," said Roberto, looking at Aurora.

"Yeah, lots," added Aurora, shifting her gaze from Robert to the other couple and then to the front of the room, waiting to hear from the fellow, who was clearly eager to keep talking. As he indeed did, a few seconds later.

"Well, my friends, 'quality of life', if you'll allow me to call it that . . ."

"Sure, sure, of course," all four said, acting as if they had known each other all their lives.

"'Quality of life', friends," he slowly continued, "does not just mean living comfortably. Materialistic values have been substituted by *postmaterialist* values. And what does that mean? That we human beings here in Europe aspire to something higher than economic wellbeing and personal security. Our interests point elsewhere – in the direction that has doubtless brought you here and has permitted us to meet each other this afternoon: study! A desire for self-actualisation! Therein lies the importance of this Great Encyclopaedia, which is marching hand in hand with the quiet revolution that, as I've just said, is rewriting all the rules."

Aurora began to feel an urgent need to own those 20 volumes. She thought of how much they really could learn at home. Unable to restrain herself, she grabbed her husband's arms and whispered "Think of how many things we could learn, and how much we could teach our children in the future, Roberto."

"Auro," said Roberto without taking his eyes off the front of the room, as if he were saying, "Yes, dear, yes, dear," even though it was clear that the answer was no.

And so, Aurora assumed that it was impossible.

"The things that pop into my head!" She turned back to face the front.

This hint of weakness was detected with great enthusiasm by the salesman though he kept the knot in his stomach to himself. He kept on talking – even more emphatically, if that were possible.

"As for the successful men and women of the age of competition, it turns out they were all plastic! They burned up and burned out too easily! They had lots of resources," he rubbed his fingers together frenetically to signify cash without naming it, "but they had no inner resources," he went on, smiling at his own witticism. "For all that they proclaimed the triumph of appearance over reality, the truth is that the years of the new century point in the opposite direction. Up with connoisseurs! Long live intellectual capital! Aren't you all with me?"

Total silence.

"Now is the time for reading books without fear. Thank you very much."

"Are we supposed to clap?" Aurora whispered to Roberto.

"No, doesn't look like it," he replied, looking at the other couple, who were already getting up.

"But it was all right, wasn't it?" Aurora asked.

They won their wristwatch and laughed all the way along the Casa de Campo after they left the Navarra pavilion, where the event had taken place. They had ice creams and then went for a boat ride. Roberto manned the oars with his customary dexterity. Every now and then he glanced down at the quartz-and-steel watch on his left wrist, which reflected the glare from the sun and the water.

Aurora charged towards the watch and towards him.

Now she didn't have him, but the watch was in her hands, though she would have to look down to see it. She reached the end of the corridor, holding the watch loosely in her fingers, level with her hips. The laughter from the lake made her feel sad: that was one of the last Saturdays they had spent together. It wasn't that Aurora hadn't laughed since, but never again as she had then, when the two of them were about to fall into the water.

Large and masculine, steel and quartz; it needed no batteries (or at least that's what they'd said), but after three years stuck inside another, larger clock it had relaxed into a sweet slumber.

She took her small watch off her right wrist and put it in the box for the other one, her husband's watch. Then she placed it inside the clock and bid it a fond farewell.

"You're not small; you're a big watch, big and beautiful. I'll be back for you, but let me leave you here for a while to rest from all that washing-up liquid."

With Roberto's watch on her wrist, she didn't feel more stylish or more in keeping with the dawn of the new millennium, but, as that chic gent from the telly had reminded her, she had attained two things without spending any money: first, a minimalist, robust quartz watch, given to her just before the end of the century; and second, the same fellow had given her, for no money of her own, a beautiful, small watch, the likes of which you could never find – an antiquarian object, a priceless object . . . and magically economical. And despite all this, one morning her boyfriend had told her that, in time, she would find herself wearing prettier watches.

And now she had found one, sleeping inside the clock. Wearing it, she went to prepare the green beans that she had set aside for dinner.

First, she ate a leisurely breakfast. She didn't want the company of the television or the radio. Silence was better, so that Roberto's watch could wake up peacefully on Aurora's right wrist. And while she drank her milk and ate her Chiquilín biscuits, she glanced down at it, just as Roberto had done that afternoon on the Casa de Campo lake. Yes, it had started working again, though she hadn't noticed it at first; the second hand was so slender that, fast as it went, it was scarcely visible.

She should also start working. She was aware of her need to find a job and get out of the house.

"It's a new phase, and you're here with me, my love," she told the watch, feeling more alive now.

When she spread cream on her face and body after the shower, she moved her hands as if she were shaking a pair of maracas, just so that the watch would feel the movement and its mechanism would be charged with a desire to keep working, day and night. "I don't want it to think that, when I'm sleeping tonight, it has returned to the darkness of the clock," she told herself.

"You get to work, and I'll get to work myself," she said, looking at the watch in the mirror while watching and listening to herself talk to a samba beat.

Then she surprised herself by starting to dance. To tell the truth, she didn't surprise herself. She loved dancing. First went her right wrist and her face; then her legs and her left wrist followed. No music was to be heard, but it must have been a bit Caribbean, because Aurora moved her hips ceaselessly, and when she sat down she was truly tired, groaning *Ayyyy*, like they did when the dances ended at the summer fiestas in her village, San Clemente de Quintás, up in the province of Ourense.

CHAPTER III

At the age of 25, the girl at checkout counter number three in the Mediodía supermarket was beginning her working life with a demanding work day, even though it was a split shift. For the first time, Fany had got up earlier than her neighbour. Aurora was still eagerly (and unsuccessfully) searching her pantry for a package of ground coffee, still unable to take her eyes off her quartz watch, when Fany was allowed a short break for the mid-morning snack.

"The main thing is to start," Fany was listening to her mother say, early on that first day. "That's how you carve out a future for yourself, with an eye out for how you stay ahead of the game when things turn sour. You stash away some funds, bit by bit, and then, tomorrow or the day after, you'll have a little something to fall back on if you're taken ill – or you want to buy, say, a dozen roast chestnuts when the weather turns chilly.

"When you're older, you'll understand," her mother went on, while Fany, who was nearly 26, stared at her, slack-jawed.

"Old people like to keep a few roasted chestnuts in their pockets and feel that they've got a reason for going out when they leave home in the morning," Fany's mother insisted. "More important than eating the chestnuts, it's knowing you can buy some without having to scrimp. Just look at your grandfather: there he is, the envy of his card partners. One day he'll have his pockets full, there he goes, eating chestnuts; the next day, maybe he'd rather have pistachios; the day after, he might want a spot of milk with a dash of cognac at the bar . . . So there you go, Fany: be autonomous and independent, like your grandfather."

Now here she was, freezing to death, starting at the bottom of the promotional ladder for checkout operators in the Mediodía supermarket chain. Checkout number three, stationed between the frozen foods and the exit door.

She soon learned her first reflex: when the bank delayed in accepting the customer's credit card, even for a moment, it was the perfect time to rub her hands together. That was enough for her to recover the warmth she had left behind by getting up at six-thirty in the morning, dragged away from her narrow bed and her metre-wide eiderdown quilt and the butterfly-winged pillow that her mother had bought on sale at Sepu.

It was also the perfect time to start wondering what she was doing here.

The truth is that she had grown used to living within her means during the time since she'd finished her course at the Institute and the two years of beauty studies at a Centre for New Professions. As for her aspirations, she had none left to fulfil; she had accomplished them all: she had listened to her CDs, thanks to trades with her friends, so many times she didn't need to tape them – she knew them all by memory; in their absence, she had the radio, which was all hers after her mother finished listening to Iñaki Gabilondo in the kitchen; the computer (which she had won in a speed writing contest sponsored by the Fnac chain, and which she had brought upstairs to Aurora's flat the day before) usually filled the central space of her room, and with it she wrote short stories that she stored on the machine's hard drive – that way she saved on printer ink and paper; she borrowed her books from the district public library; and for the rest, she made a little money when she sold things in the shop of some friends who sold recycled goods, second-hand clothes, and goods on behalf of charities.

She used the money she made to buy clothes from the same shop. Besides, they gave her a 20 per cent discount. In this way, she was able to buy a cool pair of jeans or a jersey, and still have something left to pay for a whiskey and soda if her friends from the Institute or her mates from beautician school called on her.

"But who pays for the potatoes?" her mother constantly asked.

"She's always harping on the same story," Fany thought between shivers. "If this wind keeps up, I won't make it to summer," she added out loud to her workmate at the next checkout. "Here I am, stuck next to the door, and with this cold on my back, I'm going to come down with the flu . . ."

"Albertooooo! Go look up the price for the underwear, it's not coming up," yelled Montse, the girl at checkout counter number one. The longer the line of customers grew, the more she panicked when a price was missing; she couldn't help it.

"*Albertooooo!*" The answer was too slow in coming.

"Just leave it, don't worry," said the client, "I'll come back for it some other day."

"Should I take it off your bill, then? Should I tell them to stop checking for the price?" the checkout girl asked with an annoyed expression.

"Yeah, sure."

And he left.

Fany saw him walk past her, but she could barely lift her head. A piece of salmon and a packet of sesame seed crackers that should have been a man's property by now refused to be bought. The credit card gave no sign of life.

"I think that guy with the salmon realised it was my first day," Fany said later, when they were closing up the shop.

"Are you an idiot?" Montse asked, while she straightened the cartons of skimmed milk. Night had already fallen. "You can't imagine how many blokes come in here without any dough. And they're the first ones to buy the most expensive brands of olive oil, fuck it! Even though they don't have enough to pay for a pat of butter. We've seen it all here!"

"I bet that guy didn't have a penny in the bank." Marga, the other checkout operator, butted in on the conversation.

"The truth is, he was really nice. He said that if there were any problems, he'd pay for it in cash, and I thanked him," Fany said.

"That's too sweet!" checkout operators one and two laughed at the same time.

Fany had no idea what her workmates meant by their laughter. She was the outsider, didn't understand. "I've got my head in the clouds, I don't get anything," she thought angrily.

"Are the almond tarts supposed to go over by the cereal boxes?" Fany asked the supervisor, who was walking around the store straightening boxes, in order to change the subject.

"No, no. All that stuff goes back to the warehouse today, because we'll be bringing out the Christmas items next week."

"Get along with you, sweetheart, to the warehouse. That'll do you more good than you could believe," said operator number one, with her eye on the clock.

"We're cloooosed!" Montse ranted at the exit door, through which she herself could not yet exit.

"It's just," it seemed that the person standing outside was trying to say, expressing herself more with her raised arms than through words.

"We're *clooooooosed!*" Montse gritted her teeth so hard it seemed that they would break right there as she turned her back to the door.

"It's just that," the woman was still insisting.

"No, fuck it. It's eight-thirty!" Montse yelled, pointing at her watch with her index finger and then making an X with her arms at the woman standing outside. "Can't you read the sign?" she added. "What a pain! These over-privileged cows always have to show up like this!"

Fany had barely lifted her eyes when she saw her neighbour

from the fifth floor – her friend, actually. Aurora, "the philoso-
pher", as she liked to call her, was standing out there in the
winter chill, waving from the street, hoping to catch Fany's
attention.

And that was when Fany learned, not her first reflex (which
she had discovered by rubbing her hands together while standing at the checkout), but the first real lesson of working life at
the Mediodía supermarket chain: "If I'm a checkout operator,
I'm a checkout operator, and it's hard enough as it is for me to
find a space for myself in this tribe without, on top of it all,
having to let them see me lend a hand to some over-privileged
cow of a neighbour," she thought in a flash, not taking the time
to observe that she couldn't recognise herself in her own
comments.

Checkout operator number three hid from the woman who
was waiting for her. Fany quickly told herself, "I've done plenty
for her by typing up her whole c.v. yesterday. Enough's enough."
She ducked into the warehouse with the almond tarts and didn't
come back out until she had finished with all the boxes of
Christmas nougats, sparkling wine, and holiday shortbread, and
it was a bit past nine-fifteen.

On the night of her first day at work, her nightmares would
revolve around putting things in order, and the disorder in her
mind; the heavy packages, the boxes, her cash box and the credit
cards.

But before she got back to her narrow bed, her metre-wide
eiderdown quilt, and her butterfly-winged pillow, she met Aurora
on the street; she was still waiting there, radiant and freezing,
sitting on a pile of empty orange crates. Her hands looked like
those of checkout operator number three at nine in the morning: they were the same vermilion red as everyone's hands in
small supermarkets. She felt how cold Aurora's hands were by
their contrast to the heat of the roasted chestnuts that her fifth-
floor neighbour offered her: nice and toasty, just the way she
liked them.

"How was your first day?" Aurora asked her, not noticing the tears that streamed from her eyes and the watering of her nose from the cold.

CHAPTER IV

Viewed from behind, they looked like sisters. Today they even looked similar in height. Aurora, slightly taller, was hunched with cold and the discomfort of sitting on a pile of orange crates for an hour. She was actually stooping over as she walked, though she didn't notice. Nor did Fany realise that she had added two centimetres; by stretching her back, she reached the same height as her walking companion, who still offered her a supporting though not a very stable arm. Which Fany appreciated, because it allowed her to stretch and loosen her checkout-stiffened bones.

"You really look worn out, Fany. Couldn't you have put on a little blusher at lunch time?" Aurora asked.

"At lunch time? No way."

It was the first time Fany looked at Aurora, and she saw that she looked terrible; she thought as much, but didn't say so directly to her friend. Aurora had put so much care into touching up her eyes with silver-hued liner that Fany felt obliged to remain silent.

"She must have spent a long time putting on her make-up, and there I was, turning my back on her, even hiding from her. No, I couldn't ever tell her," Fany reflected once more, on this long November day. Instead, she squeezed her companion's arm in a gentle plea for pardon; but Aurora's arm felt like a block of senseless wood, or worse, a lump of iron that had been left out in the cold.

"You must be freezing. Were you waiting out here for a long time?" asked Fany, clumsily attempting to disguise her guilt.

"Well, today is your day, Fany," said Aurora, oblivious to everything. "I'm just anxious to hear how it all went." She was shivering.

"They had all us new girls go to a meeting. There's actually plenty of us, because there are so many of these Mediodía shops. They took us to a bar – the one that looks like a shrine, have you seen it? Yeah, one of those winter bars, over on Delicias. They bought us a bit of lunch there, since it was our first day, and they talked about how important our work was and they asked us where our families usually go shopping."

"Why? Did they give you points for that when they hired you?"

"For what?"

"For your families being customers already."

"No, that was the first time they asked me about it."

"Then I don't get it. It must be that they want all your relatives to start being regular Mediodía customers."

"Bollocks, I bet that's it . . ."

"What's with that?"

"What's with what?"

"With the bollocks – I've never heard you say that before."

"I dunno, I must've picked it up from Tomás, the fruit guy," Fany said absentmindedly. "You know, I bet that's it, I really bet it is, because next they poured us a glass of cider for a toast; and they took us aside in groups to tell us that we should have our parents jot down their names when they visit us at our checkout counters. To tell you the truth, I didn't really understand what they were getting at, but they told me that they'd explain it all later on, because there was too much to learn the first day."

"Anyway, tallying up the receipts must be the most important thing, I would think," Aurora said.

"The supervisor does that at the end of the day, while we're cleaning and clearing up all the merchandise, on the shelves out here and in the warehouse."

"Now I understand why you're pulling that long face. Want to go for a drink?"

"Some other time, Aurora. My mother will be waiting up for me, to hear the whole story, and anyway, I want to get to bed as soon as I can. I have to get up again at six-thirty tomorrow, you know."

"I missed you at breakfast today, even though we wouldn't have had any coffee . . . I'll just have to get used to it, now that you're becoming a working woman."

"There's a special offer on coffee in the Mediodía shops right now, Aurora."

Aurora smiled. "What do you know about the price of coffee?"

"What do you know?"

"Me? Not a thing. I don't even remember what I paid for it last time," Aurora replied, a bit dejectedly.

"You sent off your c.v., didn't you? You'll see how quickly the agency gets back to you," Fany said, hitting the right note.

"Yes, I posted it last night."

They reached the front door. "Time to climb," they'd say each time they had to walk up the stairs, which was every day, since there was no lift in the building. "At least you get to stop at the first floor, Fany, but me . . ." said Aurora as she climbed on up the stairs.

When she was already at the third storey, Fany shouted up to her from the first floor landing, through the atrium in the middle of the staircase: "Aurora!"

"What?"

"Keep the computer for now! I'll lend it to you for a few days. After all, I'll barely be home."

"But I don't know how it works!"

"Just play around with it until you can get it to help you learn. The only thing is to give it the secret key to start it.

It'll ask you for the key, and then you're off, take it from there."

"What key?"

"It's a word. Type *fanypitt* when it asks for the secret pass-something. Passport, password or something like that. It's my first name, spelled just like it sounds, plus *pitt* with two t's at the end."

"Like Brad Pitt?"

"Yeah – not bad, huh? It asks for a key with eight letters, so that's why I put in both names. We fit together perfectly." Fany smiled, resting against the wall of the landing. It was the first time that day she had stretched her lips into a pleasant expression.

"I'd prefer *harrison*," Aurora said suddenly, a few storeys higher.

"Like Harrison Ford?"

"He's got eight letters all by himself; he doesn't even need the last name."

"But did you see him in *Random Hearts*? Forget it, Aurora."

"I know! *Miguelbosé*, like that, all bunched together."

"But count it – does *miguelbosé* have eight letters? Isn't it more like ten?"

Fany's mental agility came to her in spite of her exhaustion; when that spark went off inside her head, there was no beating her – not with logic, not with maths, not with the most unlooked for twists of reason. Aurora knew this well.

"Well, then . . . *dominguín*."

"Still one letter too many," Fany said quickly, before she had even heard the whole name. "Whose computer is it, anyway? Just type *fanypitt* and that's that. Look, good night, OK? Why don't you type up another c.v., and when you finish I'll look it over to see if you understood the programme."

"Good night, get some rest." And Aurora climbed on up, still thinking.

CHAPTER V

Madrid, 2 November 2000
(Or November 2, 2000? Sorry, but today
I don't have anybody helping me,
so I am uncertain right from the start.)

Dear Sir:
Dear Madam:
Dear Sir or Madam:
To the Staff of the Talento Temporary Recruitment
Agency, Tetuán Office:

I think I can start now, since I haven't left anybody out; well, nobody that I know of, and that is all of you. That is, what I mean to say is, since I do not know you, it seems like there are whole crowds of you, many more than in the other letter that I sent to you more than a month ago. As I was saying, it must be because I am alone today and everything seems a bit of an uphill battle.

Do you remember Fany, the girl I mentioned in the other letter? She is still working as a checkout operator in the Mediodía supermarket. She's caught a couple of colds already, but there she is, strong as ever, and she hasn't missed a day's work no matter how high her temperature has been. Today, for example, her mother told me on the stairs that she went to work with her face looking greenish-yellow . . .

But forgive me. I should ask you, first of all, whether you remember me. I am Aurora, and I live in the Tetuán district, not far from your agency. Do you remember now? Forgive me, suddenly I'm blushing from head to toe; it makes me a bit sad to think that you don't know anything about me. And really, why should you? You must have piles of work to do. But the thing is, today I'd like to have a bit of company. Don't get me wrong; I don't know how to explain it to you, but today is one of those days when a person would like everybody to know who she is, to be recognised, and more than that: to be remembered.

Do you remember me now? Forgive me for asking you so directly. I don't want to make you feel uncomfortable.

I'm feeling a little *muixona*. I mean, a little homesick – that's how they say it up in my village, San Clemente de Quintás, in the province of Ourense, not far off the main road to Lugo. My Aunt Domi just called me from there. She says that the village is bustling now. She also says I should visit, because it's almost time for the *Magosto*. Do you know what that is? It's the chestnut harvest, and all the villagers throw parties, they break out the brandy, and they thread raisins and dried fruit on ribbons that they string up to decorate their houses. Also, Domi knows that it's near the time when I got the phone call from the North Madrid train station, and so – one of life's coincidences – I can never keep calm when the *Magosto* comes around.

It seems like I'm so busy the rest of the year, what with helping the Ecuadorians and taking care of their kids, that I manage to distract myself. But when it's the anniversary of the death of Roberto, my husband, I'm always off on a train somewhere. I can't bear to hear the phone ring on the tenth of November in my house on Bravo Murillo street.

So I'll go and see the commotion in my village.

Anyway, don't think I'm getting off the subject, because, even though I'm one of those girls who talk a lot, I am capable of synthesising things. I was telling you two things: first, that I am a person who needs more affection than most, if such a thing is possible, and please forgive my vanity. And second, that I want to go back to my village for a few days to see if I can rejuvenate myself with a little of what I'm saying I need. But then I suddenly started thinking that I don't want to betray you, because I've asked you urgently in several letters to find me a job (as you know, I would like to be the caretaker of a peaceful building, if possible). So I'm not just going to disappear as if it didn't matter, and make it look like I'm not really interested.

That is what's behind this new letter: I want to let you know that, if there is no objection, I will be out of town for a week, even though I still don't even know when I will go to buy the ticket. But it'll be soon. I'll jot down my phone number by hand at the end of the page, just in case you want to give me a ring, since we all know that the post doesn't always get the job done, especially at this time of year, when all sorts of things start getting complicated: the traffic, the post, the price of grapes, everything in general.

You work in this neighbourhood, and you're in the office until late every day, so you must have noticed what Bravo Murillo street is like at night. I can see you all, worn to the bone, wrapping up for the day, when I'm walking back from volunteering at an NGO that takes care of the Ecuadorian kids in the neighbourhood. You must have seen that before long this street is going to look like Quito; better for them, though, because that way they'll feel more at home. I don't know if you've noticed that they sell *cassava* on Sundays in the little open market on Marqués de Viana street now; but the mothers of the kids I sometimes play with in the afternoons tell me that the *cassava* they sell here is dry, not like the fresh *yuca* in their country.

Oh, but you probably aren't even around here on Sundays, now I think about it! You must be home with your families, going for Sunday outings in your own parts of town, and I bet you don't have the least desire to see this street again – that's what Monday and Tuesday and the rest of the working week are for.

Sometimes I feel like bringing you a bit of – well, I won't say *cassava* now, but maybe some fresh dates, which don't stain, and you can eat them just fine without having to leave your desks. My offer to make you a tortilla still stands; the thing is, I'm overwhelmed by the thought of how many of you there are – I wouldn't know how many eggs to add to the frying pan. Why does it seem to me that there are so many of you today? Don't think for a second that I would go back on my promise just because of that, no . . . But, it seems like there are many more of you than I guess we used to have over for dinner when Roberto was alive; my mother-in-law was always asking us if we were going to have to take out a second mortgage, because of all the invitations we extended to neighbours, to relatives, to a few friends . . .

I love it when I'm caught up in the thick of it, as you can see. And here I am, all alone.

I'd rather say alone than widowed. At any rate, I mention this to you in case you find it useful as complementary information to the first letter. I live alone, terribly in love with my husband who is no longer with me, or with anyone else, you know. It's that he died. He's far from me, but close to my life; we didn't have children; we didn't have enough time. I'm sane, not crazy, just still a bit in love.

It's getting near the date when they called me from Renfe, where he worked, and I relive it all over again. Isn't that a contradiction, to relive death? It's going to be three years soon that I've been missing him.

"You're each other's better halves, you fit just right," my mother-in-law told me when she gave me Roberto's medallion from his first communion; and we hadn't even set a wedding date then or anything.

"Better halves? No way, love," said Maribel, my Aunt Domi's friend, and I think she was really putting her foot in it; but she's always been one of those big-mouths who don't mean badly – at least, that's what my aunt told me, so that I'd get over my anger. Domi always says that her friend has simple ideas, but not an ounce of malice. I don't know what you must think about it; the thing is, Maribel said, right out loud, "Don't go around telling the girl things like that, about better halves and being born for each other and such rot. She shouldn't go around believing all that . . ."

"Maribel!" shouted the other villagers who were standing nearby. They repeated, at the same time, "Maribel!" but they didn't add anything else, and so she kept talking.

"You bet, that's just what happens to us women, we start believing in being born for someone and being someone's better half, for Christ's sake. Then they dump you, and then what? You're unbalanced from then on. Am I right or not? And if not, let them tell that to your sister," she said, making things worse by looking at my Aunt Domi.

My mother was abandoned by my father before I was even born, but she never acted like she had been dumped. I don't know if I do or not.

(The only thing I know about my father is that he also lives in Madrid and that he is a bigwig in some Ministry. Even if we ran into each other in the street, we wouldn't recognise each other! In order to recognise somebody you have to have seen him before, at least once, and that's never happened with us. He left me, a tadpole in my mother's belly, during a holiday one Holy Week when his parents, who would be my grandparents now, took a holiday in my village. They never returned to San Clemente – neither he, nor anyone in his family.)

"He fits you like a glove," my friends also said (more acquaintances than friends; I don't even know where any of them are now) when we talked about Roberto. Ignacio the tobacconist told me they'd turn green with envy whenever they saw us sharing a cool drink at Joaquín's bar.

As for me, I kept a steady head.

Roberto explained his theory about it to me. He said that there was no such thing as fitting like a glove, or being somebody's better half; he said he saw the two of us as a puzzle with lots of pieces, where one piece gets matched with another, and then those two open up a path for more and more pieces to follow.

The first gift he gave me was a 300-piece puzzle. Of a train. The things life hands you, right? A train!

And that's where Roberto's gift is, in the North Madrid train station. I gave it away to his workmates, and they keep it there in the traffic control room, glued and framed and varnished. No doubt it's still shiny and new.

I wear his watch. It's a big quartz watch, and it works like a charm. It weighs down my right wrist a little, to tell the truth; while I'm typing this it feels like I'm lifting weights. But the minimalist things we use at the turn of the century have to be like this. Robust. With lots of character, even if it hurts.

Today must be my day to try out new things: the watch I just mentioned, and this deluxe computer, which my neighbour Fany lent me. The poor dear doesn't have a free minute to work on it, so she has lent it to me.

They gave it to her, or rather, she won it in a speed writing contest sponsored by Fnac. I still remember, when the day came for her to go to the award ceremony, the poor girl didn't even know what to wear.

In the fashion programmes on TV, they always tell you what people are wearing – which colours are in, how long skirts should be, how to cut your hair; but what about how you should dress when you go out to eat? When you go to the theatre, even if it's a half-price Wednesday show? What you should wear when somebody invites you to their house for a snack in the middle of the afternoon? Forget it. They're certainly not going to give you advice about how to dress if you're invited to an award ceremony, where you turn out to be the Grand Prize winner and there's going to be reporters there and everything. Forget it, they don't tell you a thing. I told her to wear black or brown, but the weather was already getting hot then, and I didn't have the slightest idea whether she should be wearing stockings or not. What a mess.

She finally picked out a rather nice pair of trousers, and a few other items, which she borrowed for a few hours (though I shouldn't be telling you this) from her friends at a second-hand clothing store: a very chic blouse – just imagine, even second-hand it cost a fortune, so what must the owner have paid for it? If that lady had seen Fany she would have realised how great the blouse looked. She would've wanted to buy it back again! The blouse was muslin, and a bit ostentatious for Fany's style, but she managed to tone it right down with a lilac scarf. Fany always wears something lilac; all her friends know it, so they let her be faithful to her principles on such an important day. And for free. They matched the loan of the blouse with that of the scarf.

She dedicated the prize to her friends. That's all she said at the microphone, that she dedicated it to them, and she winked at them. From their seats in the second row, they watched her, looking so pretty and happy. Later Fany told me that the dedication was also for me, but I can't see myself in that picture, no matter how I look at it.

I was sitting there, half camouflaged, like it or not, behind a curtain.

Then something strange occurred; something that none of us who were there in the audience could ever have expected or imagined. Even though she had won a prize for speed-writing a short story, what she really wanted to do was read a poem that she had written a few months earlier – a poem she later told me had given her a lot of trouble.

It all happened very fast. No sooner had she taken the microphone than she broke into the poem, with that solid voice that you only hear from headmistresses when they are talking over the loudspeakers in the school playground. And then, wham. Like when you decide to dive head-first into the river, no matter how freezing cold the water is. Fany plunged in. Slowly.

> . . . *Later, morning will be his absence*
> *your dawnlit delay, a memory*
> *his portrait, lost in the mirroring*
> *lure of your*
> *tears . . .*

Her parents were dumbfounded by her self-assurance. Disquieted by her sadness.

The organisers of the event were also a bit unnerved. (I didn't find out until a few weeks later that Fany had written this poem one night when she saw me looking very sad. Since then, though we're completely unlike each other, my neighbour has been a great friend of mine, because only someone who can touch your soul with the tips of her fingers deserves your unrestrained friendship.)

The hall fell totally silent, out of sheer uncertainty.

Don't you think it must take nerves of steel to suddenly impose a slowness and a seriousness that nobody anticipated or, perhaps, appreciated? I think that the only people who understand writers are their readers, people like me who like to read and to mull over what we read. Not even other writers have the capacity to absorb their meaning, because anybody who writes pays more attention to his own readers than to other writers, and let's not even mention the readers of other writers.

Fany is a writer, of course. I realised it that day, when she recited her poem up there, in that silence, without rushing anything, until a certain moment when her face became radiant, as if she were a great diva, and she raised the paper with her verses on it up towards the ceiling with the ineffable verve of utter contentment. That was the end of her performance.

Nobody had had any intention of applauding in that atmosphere – why lie about it? – but her heroic gesture sparked an ovation. Fany, with her lilac scarf, had entered writers' heaven. Who would have said that she was the same woman as the first-floor neighbour who cried because she had a run in her tights – the black tights that she wore under her own trousers, below that ostentatious, borrowed blouse? But was this Fany, in her glory up there on stage, really the same woman as the one who had been babbling about her insecurities, unsure of what she should wear to a literary award ceremony where she turned out to be the absolute winner?

Fany laughed about it all, with the confidence that her brown, well-worn platform shoes gave her – the shoes, and her quick brain; her shrewd and patient mind. They gave her the computer right there, the same computer I'm using now, because – you know how things go – even though Fany is the writer, and she's learned massage therapy, and she's an expert beautician in many branches of the trade, she works as a checkout operator, as I've mentioned before, and she doesn't have time to do anything. Meanwhile, I don't have any degrees or certificates at all, but I do have lots of time, so I am a reader; I learn a lot from books, and whenever an opportunity arises, I scatter the ideas I learn. Just like the supervisor at the Mediodía supermarket, who, Fany tells me, scatters crumbs as he talks during their fifteen-minute snack break! Naturally, that's because they don't have enough time; they can eat, or they can talk. My grandmother told me long ago: "You can't sip and spit at the same time, Auro."

I hope Fany doesn't have to share her snack break with him when the shop offers them crumb cake. Pardon the joke.

My point is that I tend to scatter the bits that stick in my memory. As for the rest, I'm a good worker at whatever I try my hand.

But what I want is a job as the caretaker of a peaceful building. Please excuse my insistence.

Allow me to stress that I already have learned how to operate a computer, simply by using one; all you have to do is look at this letter, which I am writing today without Fany's help. I mention this in case it's of any use; I don't know what qualifications caretakers must have these days; maybe in the bigger buildings they require you to know about computers – you know how things are; the husband of a woman here in the neighbourhood was sacked from his cleaning job in a hospital because he didn't know . . . I don't remember what, but I think it was exactly this, how to use a computer.

Do you also have passwords on your computers? I know Fany's, but of course I can't tell you what it is, because it's secret. If I could have chosen any eight-letter word, I would have picked *aurobosé*; the thing is, I don't know if they allow accent marks on these passports, and *aurobose* without the accent mark doesn't say anything to me. What I mean is that, when it comes to punctuation, I pay close attention to detail. I mention this in case you take it into consideration.

I believe that c.v.s (or do you spell it c.v.'s?) are supposed to be short and to tell a lot of things in a few lines. As for myself, however, I write a lot and I get the impression that I haven't managed to give you many clues about who I am. Next time I'll try to improvise some new ways to get to the same goal: a job.

Sir; Madam; All of You: I give you my sincere best wishes, and in case you don't call, you should know that I understand this means you agree with my absence, even though we are, I believe, in the thick of a search for work. Therefore I would like to express, in advance, my deepest gratitude.

Aurora Ortiz

CHAPTER VI

"Aurora?"

"Hello, speaking. What's up, Fany?"

"Er, well, it's just that I saw how you said goodbye when you left. I said to myself, I'm going to find her in her village, because I'm sure that's where she's gone. But, come on, you keep a person guessing, love."

"But it's impossible to ever get hold of you! You're never around, day or night. When do you get off work?"

"Around nine, but I usually go out to eat something with my workmates from the supermarket, and then I go for a few beers with el Tomás, the guy who tends the fruit counter behind my checkout. If I don't take those breaks . . . What's the matter, are you angry?" Fany's words came tumbling out, one after another.

"No, I was just thinking . . . Why do you call him *el Tomás*? Why not just plain Tomás?"

"Well, he says it makes him stand out, you know, and he likes that. And what difference does it make?"

"But do you like him?"

"Of course, you know, but I'll tell you all about it later. I'm not going to stand here and blab about it over the phone. I'll tell you later."

"You sound happy."

"Hey, and you're not too sad, are you? I'm sending you hugs

and kisses, you know. I remembered today was the anniversary of Roberto's death, but you shouldn't let it get you down. We both know you're a tough cookie, eh, Aurora?"

"Just now I was watching the clouds pass by from the balcony. I love the chill air in my village. You can sit inside at home and watch the sun spread into everything, but you go outside and realise that the silly thing has been tricking you. It's so cold here, Fany! I'm at my Aunt Domi's, you know."

"When are you going to come down from the clouds and get back here?"

"But then we won't even bump into each other on the stairs, so what do you care! I just got here today. I don't know, I told the agency that I'd be here for a week, since they're processing my . . ."

"Hey, they called me. Did you have anything to do with it?"

"I didn't give them your phone number . . ."

"No, I mean they wrote to me. About an interview. Because it looks like there's the possibility of covering somebody's maternity leave in a beauty parlour. But how did they know my address? I hope you didn't send them a c.v. in my name, girl, because I'm doing fine! I'll bash you, I will. Was it you? I haven't been helping you with your c.v. for a long time. Don't you go around telling my story everywhere, all right?" Fany bombarded her with these questions almost all at once.

"I don't know, I'm confused."

"Well, it might have just been the people at the beauty school. I'm supposed to go to the agency next door. I'll see what I can do. Maybe I won't go. For now, I'll tell them OK, the interview lady can count on me. I don't know what they need to ask me questions for. Anyway, we could do it at breakfast, since I can't skip work at the checkout; or maybe some Sunday . . . Well, Auro, have fun up there without the traffic. Don't you miss the computer? It's all yours when you come back, OK. You know that."

"Have you written anything?"

"Nothing. I never deal with letters now, Aurora, just numbers, bills and credit cards. Good thing I've got Tomás here. Maybe I'll write a verse for him. I've had a couple of things tossed in the computer for months now, worthless little scribblings. You could take a peek at them, if you like.

"But you don't have the computer with you – I'm an idiot!" Fany went on. "Naturally, you could have taken it with you, but maybe you should look into it up there, because the other day I heard at the supermarket that there's lots of computers out in the villages so that way people can surf the Internet. I think people in the villages do a lot of computer shopping. Books, for instance, things like that. Take advantage of it while you're in Ourense, and do some surfing, Aurora. Oh, what a fool I'm being! Don't pay any attention to me. All I do is talk nonsense, and then I get an attack of the giggles without knowing why. I think I'm a little taken by that Tomás, Aurora. Hey, give us a kiss, because my mother's going to kill me – this is turning into a conference."

"Bye, Fany. Thanks for calling. And good luck with the interview."

"What interview? Oh, the beauty parlour. Sure, sure. I can't remember when it was supposed to be. I'll have to look at the letter."

CHAPTER VII

Feeling upset and losing your appetite are easier to bear in water. Aurora had come down from the clouds to answer the phone and then, after talking with Fany, she got into the bathtub to soak her disappointments. Fortunately, she didn't have to stop being up in the clouds. Her Aunt Domi's bathtub stood on the great, covered wooden balcony overhanging the orchard. It was what turned this old house in a little village in the province of Ourense into a heavenly palace.

The bathtub was placed squarely in the middle of childhood, facing straight into the sun that fell on the chestnut trees every afternoon at bath time.

"That girl spends so much time looking at the sun that she'll end up short-sighted, if not blind," Ignacia, her grandmother, used to say when she accompanied her daughter and grand-daughter at bath time.

"Not at all, Mamá. By the time the sun reaches the orchard, it can't do any harm. It's just coming to say goodbye, and that doesn't hurt anybody," Pura, Aurora's mother, would reply.

They always remembered to be thankful for hot water. When Aurora's body was already steaming, her mother and grand-mother would start to think, with a special hilarity, about the cold of the trout rivers in the area. The question never failed: "Can you *imagine* getting in the *river* now?" they'd ask slowly, with freezing voices, while their fingers ran up Aurora's arm.

"Mamaaaa!" All three would laugh at their imaginary shivers – just imagining them was enough to kill you – and they'd feel nothing but gratitude for the hot water and for the sun that was bidding them goodbye from the other side of the window panes.

The water made them feel at peace. Heaven came all by itself.

But the water also had its curative powers.

When she was tiny, before she even crawled, and barely had her first two pairs of teeth, Aurora had screamed whenever attempts were made to feed her puréed cabbage or spinach. She never wanted vegetables, no matter what colour they were. Mashed vegetables flew up almost to the ceiling, rebounded, and splattered all over the table.

If she'd had a father, he would probably have slammed his fist down on the table at suppertime and said, "For crying out loud, girl, that's enough complaining about your food!" Which is exactly what her grandfather said, but virtually without any force, for he spoke so softly. But when her grandmother Ignacia came in carrying a washbasin full of water, her crying stopped. Aurora began splashing the water with her little fingers, and when she smiled, she accepted heaped spoons without complaint.

From that day forth, the water basin had a place at their table. The plate, the spoon, the bib, the glass of milk, even Aurora and her mother were all little more than satellites orbiting the great star: the washbasin. There were no more struggles.

For little problems, little basins; for bigger problems, more water. That was her grandmother's philosophy, though no doubt it was shared by more people than Ignacia. How many summer annoyances in the village were solved by a long stroll along the river's edge, and a happy finale of laughter in the water, complete with ducking and everything! Aurora's grandparents, with diverging ideas about life, were experts at resolving their arguments this way: long strolls on which they paid no attention at all to the rain or to how muddy the ground was along the river. All their problems flowed away there. And they never brought their problems back home with them.

Only once did they have to go as far as Lugo. They took the train, and what the river couldn't do, the beach at Las Catedrales did. After an hour on the train and two hours of talking and walking, they kissed each other on the shingle between the sea and the rocks, and returned to the village.

Domi peeked past the curtain in the living room that gave on to the balcony, and there at the other end, she saw Aurora in the bath.

"Come along, come along," Domi told César, her husband. "The girl's taking a bath. Let's leave her be." And they went back to the bar in the square, which they had just left.

Domi knew well that Aurora, who had just arrived from Madrid, always needed her baths. "She soaks everything away there in the tub. You'll see – tomorrow; today's a bad day," César's wife later told all the neighbours.

"Everything involves a process of adaptation. Whenever Auro comes from Madrid, it takes her a few hours to decontaminate herself from the city. Just imagine what life in Madrid must be like," said César.

"Well, and Roberto died three years ago today," Domi added.

"How old was Aurora? I don't remember," asked Mercedes.

"How old *is* she, you mean," said Domi's husband.

"Well, that's what I meant; it's just a manner of speaking."

"Thirty," said César. "Thirty," he repeated.

"I don't think she'll stay here long. The recruitment agency needs her there for interviews with some very important firms," Domi said in a self-assured tone. "And then, she spends what little time she has left working for an NGO, helping the children of the Ecuadorians in the district, as if the girl had nothing else to do."

"We went over there, now they're the ones coming over here. They must have heard that there's work here in Spain. See how it is . . . And then here's Aurora, looking for a job that never comes," César noted.

"That's the truth. It might be easier for her to find a job in Ecuador than in Madrid. Everybody from here can go over there, and the people from there can come here. That's what I'm always saying: we've gone mad." Gaspar joined in the conversation, though most of those present questioned his words.

"No point drawing comparisons, y'know," said César. "Anyone for a game of *mus*?"

Second change of bath water.

When the water cools down, you have to follow the ritual. Without stepping away, you put on the bathrobe, pull the plug, and say goodbye to the lukewarm water. You can't be too impatient. All the water must go. All of it. Only then can the operation begin again: the black plug back in place, bath gel under the tap, hot water on full blast, feet out of the tub so they don't get scalded, towel wrapped around your head so you won't catch a cold, and the portable heater nearby. This is also a good time to bring the radio closer and turn up the volume.

Aurora was in the middle of this process. The sun was still up, high and yellow.

She once set a record of four changes of bath water. Her fingers no longer looked like flesh when she was finished. At least, not human flesh; who could have said what her fingers might have been? Pink fat on a ham, hung up to cure after the slaughter; weightless chicken claws; curdled milk; meringue; a turkey's dewlap; strawberry-coloured soap; vanilla ice cream; a washed-out oil painting . . . That's what she had looked like. Softened.

She felt better in the second bath than in the first. The radio was playing a song from the compilation CD, *The Best of Bosé*:

> *Love, I write to you, I am a witness*
> *to everything we're losing*
> *but I'll get used to it, hard as it'll be for me . . .*
> *Give me some time, at least, and let me breathe.*

> *Making promises is not an easy art.*
> *Give me some time, at least, to say goodbye.*
> *. . . In this world that passes by*
> *with the speed of light and thought,*
> *it isn't right for me to say "I meant to do,"*
> *and even though I'd rather not, is there a doubt?*
> *For this world is passing by . . .*

She smiled for the first time that day: *aurobosé*, she recalled; the computer password that *fanypitt* wouldn't let her use. "Aurobosé," she said out loud, and it sounded as good as she thought it would. "It almost sounds like aurora borealis."

"You're my comet, my meteor shower, the whole sky," Roberto had told her one night when they were making love in the Ford Fiesta. He had never mentioned the aurora borealis before that night. "Do you know what the difference is between the aurora borealis and the aurora australis?"

"I wouldn't have a clue," she replied, pulling up her tights.

As a child, she learned about her name; as a woman, she discovered these heavenly bodies.

It was an upset at school that led her to discover what her given name meant. She must have been no older than six. She left her classroom crying and ran to the school's dining hall, where her mother was in charge of keeping order at the tables and making sure the day students ate their fill.

"Mamá! Aurea says that her name is gold but mine is just tin!"

"What's that, my dear?" Pura asked in surprise, wiping away the girl's tears.

"She says her name means gold, but mine doesn't."

"Of course it doesn't. Your name means something even nicer. It means shining, glittering, my love. It's that lovely, rosy light we see when we go to Lugo and get up really early to catch the train. All that is Aurora. You want us to look it up in the dictionary?"

That day, Aurora heard straight from her mother's own sweet-sounding voice that, in this life, what glitters is more important than gold; that brilliance is worth more than money.

After that, Aurora didn't feel belittled by Aurea.

In the dictionary, she also slowly read other meanings of her name in Spanish. The book spoke of rosy cheeks, and of a strange drink made of almond milk and cinnamon water. Aurora.

That night, mother and daughter faced one other, and asked each other, with equal enthusiasm: "*Should we make a bath of almond milk and cinnamon water?*"

"Hurrah!" shouted Aurora. That day, both of them slipped into the water, along with almonds, cinnamon, soap bubbles, and the brilliant glitter of the sun that hung in the tops of the almond trees.

She liked Aurora. She had loved her name, ever since that night of the almond and cinnamon bath. One day, she wanted to have another Aurora. With Roberto.

"But, borealis or australis?"

"Come off it, Roberto, don't be silly."

"It all depends on where you see the lights: in the southern hemisphere, you see the lights in the south, and they're attributed to electric activity. That's the aurora australis. But the aurora borealis – you see that in the northern hemisphere, and the lights are up in the north. And, of course, they're also attributed to electric activity. Is that clear?"

"Know-it-all!" Aurora shouldered him up against the handbrake. "Instead of studying for the Renfe exams, you should be studying for NASA!"

It wasn't clear at all to Aurora. What she retained in her mind was that the aurora borealis was her favourite, because it was in the north.

"What difference does it make where you see it; after all, you'd have to have a lot of luck to see it any night," she had thought. "And . . . if it ever happens, I'll be with Roberto, and he'll explain it to me."

For Aurora, the north was unattainable. It was one of the most ancient ideas that she had inherited – one of those that grow stronger, generation after generation – that the north always stays ahead of you; one step in front of where you are.

What matters is where you ask the question. There is no point in circling around and asking again, where is the north?

"You're contradicting yourself," Ignacia said her own mother reproached her when she played with these concepts.

The fact is that this congenital habit of straying, this arrhythmia in her sense of space, this absolute inability to follow the most basic co-ordinates, dogged Aurora from her first baby bath.

North was always over, away, out there, in the distance – like the sea.

There was no doubt about the fact that, as the midpoint between the washbasin on the kitchen table and the Cantabrian Sea, the bathtub had to be facing north. This thought occurred to the family when they were two steps away from the balcony; it came to them there, before the big windows overlooking the orchard.

At least that was true so long as her mother and grandparents were alive. It was her Aunt Domi, with her feet so much more firmly planted on the ground, who told her one day that there was no way the orchard could be on the north side; the boughs of the almond trees couldn't have withstood a north wind for two days. She made the remark soon after she and her husband had moved into the old family house, soon after her parents and her sister Pura had died. Aurora had gone with Roberto to Madrid, and so the old family house in Ourense had fallen to the care of Domi and César, Aurora's only remaining relatives in the village.

They had become her unconditional allies, especially Domi. Not only because Domi had kept Aurora company during her mother's illness, and had strewn the path from the old house to the church square with daisies on her wedding day; not only because Domi had made straw huts with her in the hayloft, and had treated her mosquito bites afterwards; not only because Domi had dissipated the drama of her first menstrual period, before Roberto had come into her life and when her mother was already suffering from cancer. More than anything, Aurora would give her soul for Domi because, even though she had refurbished the old house and made it all so functional, she had kept the bathtub on the balcony. And this was in spite of her aunt's discovery that the bathtub, in the middle of the bay window, far from facing north, actually took up the best view and the warmest space in the house.

Aurora moved the electric heater closer, and slipped down into the water (still hot), until it covered her up to the back of her head.

She smiled more broadly when she recalled the summer nights when little Aurora and her mother were sure they would be able to see the aurora borealis. One night after another.

"Then tomorrow you'll tell Aurea how pretty it was," her mother would say.

But they never saw it. North was the other direction, at the back of the house, above the patio, over the valley – where Domi sews now on hot summer afternoons.

Even when she was in the right spot, she never had time to see an aurora borealis with Roberto.

Nonetheless, with all of them there near the bathtub, Aurora began to feel better. She didn't need a third bath, and nor would she think about her conversation with Fany, who, without meaning to, had proved that Aurora had been wasting her time writing to the agency, a firm that had never replied to her letters but had managed to discover, by reading between the lines, that her neighbour, the checkout operator, had studied to be a beautician.

Just thinking about it, and about the tortilla and the fresh dates she had offered them, turned her stomach.

"I'll get indigestion if I think about it." She got carefully out of the bath, unaware that she had been soaking there for two and a half hours. Feeling strong again, though fragile, she wrapped herself first in the bathrobe and then in a blanket. She wrapped a towel around her head and let herself sink into a yellow hammock that was strung up next to the tub.

This was the first step: recover from the low blood pressure the hot water gave her, in the cold atmosphere, though she only felt the chill on her face.

And so, lying horizontal and wrapped up like a mummy in her Palencia blanket, she looked up at the sky and saw that, at this late hour, it was coloured with a rosy glow. A soft brilliance, like the glittering auroras at dawn she'd seen when she accompanied her mother to Lugo.

She only stopped looking up when she leaned over to turn off the radio and go back to reading *The Magic Mountain* while there was still enough light. But just when she had her finger on the radio's black button, on came the voice of Manolo Tena. It would have been impossible to keep from listening.

> *Sometimes I wish I could go to the moon with you,*
> *I wish there was no such word as never,*
> *I wish I could drink but not forget,*
> *I wish I could be happy and start it all again.*
>
> *I wish I were the sea, but all I have is foam.*
> *I wish I could go on, but all I have is foam.*
> *I can't make it without you, won't you give me a hand.*
> *All I have is doubt.*
>
> *I wish I were the sea, but all I have is foam . . .*

Again Aurora reached her hand out from her shroud, but this time she reached to the right. She leaned over far enough to gather a weightless handful of foam from the bathtub – it was as easy to gather as spreading warm butter on toast, no effort at all. The water was still lukewarm, and so was the foam. She raised it to her face and blew it so hard that the soap bubbles almost splattered against the window panes.

It was fine. Perfectly fine. If not, the foam wouldn't have gone so far.

That was another theory she had inherited from her grand-mother: when you are down in the dumps, you should blow away some foam while looking up at the ceiling; and on top of that (according to Ignacia), you should keep your head up while you watch to see where the foam falls, as if deep down you wished that, as it descended, a bit of soap would get in your eyes and the itching would give you a better excuse to cry.

However, when your blood is full of verve and vigour, you blow so hard that the foam migrates far away.

Towards the north. At full speed.

CHAPTER VIII

His name was Clemente, just like the village, San Clemente de Quintás; which was quite a coincidence, said the villagers, who had put on their Sunday best to meet the man they expected would soon become the new occupant of their parish church. They were eager to hear some new sermons.

"Well, maybe his name is the same, but that doesn't make him a saint. San Clemente's body still lies, uncorrupted, in the cemetery at Lonxo, and bear in mind that they check it every ten years and there he is, tiny but complete, with his little hands folded over his chest," said Joaquín, the bar owner.

"Maybe it's really Diego Velázquez – perhaps he came up here to die, and that's why they can't find his bones in Madrid!" A few people laughed at Blas's stab at wit.

On Sundays, the villagers habitually huddled in little groups before Mass. Without these light-hearted chats, the morning turned into a rather long haul, and so, regardless of the heat or the cold, they were never stingy with their time as they stood around in the square before passing through the squat door of their Romanesque church, the pride of the village.

"Domi and César aren't here yet – I'll wait outside for them," someone volunteered.

"And where have Maribel and her aunt got themselves? I'll wait with you," said don Ignacio, tapping a packet of Ducados cigarettes with his index finger.

The volunteers started gathering around to take full advantage of this break, for although they were all very punctual, none of them was in much of a hurry to enter the dark, dank passageway that led into the church.

Domi, who as it turns out was already waiting indoors, emerged to let the people standing around outside know.

"Hey, come on, let's go in," she announced, energetically beckoning, as if she were fanning her face on this cold winter Galician day.

"What's Domi doing there?" asked several people. "What's up?"

"Come on in! I think our new priest has arrived."

"What, is he going to start calling the roll, too? Bloody hell . . ." said don Ignacio, the tobacconist and newspaper vendor, as he stubbed out the Ducados he had just lit.

"Come on, you don't want to miss this!"

"Well, Domi's certainly worked up about it. But where's César?"

Everybody moved inside, all of them taking off gloves and scarves as they went, for the church was a bit warmer than usual on this day.

"Good Lord!" don Ignacio couldn't help blurting out under his breath.

Those who were already sitting on the benches up front turned around. They knew the exclamation had come from don Ignacio, the fellow who sold them cigarettes, newspapers, lottery tickets and lighters. They didn't want to miss the look on his face when he looked up at the altar and saw what they had seen ten minutes earlier: a young man of 30-odd years, wearing an old vestment that he must have ferreted out of the sacristy and that was too short for him; and, sticking out from under the hem, blue jeans and damp, muddy tennis shoes. In fact, he was wet all over – his hair was plastered down, as if he had just stepped out of the shower.

"He looks like he just came back from fishing, and he might have caught a trout," came a voice from one of the benches.

"But where has he come from?"

"Must have been from the river – like I say, this fellow looks like he enjoys the rivers around here."

Don Ignacio sat down. And closed his mouth, at last.

Clemente took advantage of the commotion to go back into the sacristy. He returned, drying his hair with a towel.

"Watch out, kid, or you'll catch a cold!" Domi said in ringing tones from the aisle by the third bench, and she broke into a long laugh – one of those laughs that sound like screeching to other people, but not to the person who is having a good time and wants to show it at all costs. "Oh, what a hoot!" she went on in her stiletto-heel voice, the kind that pierces your inner ear, and which had inexorably stood out above all the rest whenever the former priest, don Julián, had called on his parishioners to sing "Thee, Oh God, We Praise".

"Here you go, Domi, take this," her husband whispered, passing her a handkerchief. César had the expression that his face involuntarily wore when he felt unsettled by a new situation, and didn't yet know whether to feel happy or cross about it. He was always slow to react; just the opposite of his wife, Domi, who was so tickled that her eyes were already red from rubbing them.

"Kid, you know it gets cold here in Ourense. Don't you want a hairdryer?" Domi went on, looking up at the altar and loudly slapping her knee at her joke.

"There's a socket over there next to the Virgin, if you want to dry your hair," another woman cried out from further back.

The young man in jeans and sneakers faced the 50 citizens of the village, in no hurry to stop their murmuring. He wasn't going to use the socket, but he took advantage of looking for it to appraise the whole altarpiece; he didn't miss any detail, from top to bottom, left to right.

"Enough, let's get this over before Christmas! Who are you, anyway? The new priest, or who the devil are you? Is there going to be a Mass or not?" Don Ignacio was in a rage by now; he was beginning to wonder what he was doing here, at one end of the Romanesque church of San Clemente de Quintás, when he could have been nursing a tumbler at Joaquín's bar, not more than 50 metres away.

"I can't believe he's a real priest," Gaspar commented in a whisper to his next-door neighbour, who also sat beside him on the bench.

"Shhhh, come on, let the kid be," said Ambrosio, a fellow who never talked.

Or never had talked, until today.

Village rumour had it that Ambrosio had only opened the front door to his house on the day he said "I do" to Lidia: on their wedding day. He never opened it again, so far as the villagers knew, not even when they came to give their condolences for the death of his wife; he and she had shared their mistrust for all the rest, and even though he always kept his ears tuned to hear what everybody else was saying, he and his wife (while she was alive) maintained a stony silence whenever they were in a group. They left their comments inside, behind the closed doors of their house.

Nonetheless, his *mus* partners had begun to notice a change when, after ten years of playing cards every day at five in the afternoon, Ambrosio said to don Ignacio, just three days before Mass, "You're just pretending you have a winning hand – your cards ain't worth bugger all." Nobody wanted to show surprise, lest Ambrosio had an attack of regret, and then they'd be back to playing the way they always had. But the fact of the matter was that, at that moment, the other three were so knocked off balance that they didn't know whether they were playing *mus*, *pocha* or *cinquillo*.

But what he had done today – standing up in the middle of the church, demanding everyone's silence on behalf of whoever that was up there at the altar – so shocked his neighbours that they might well have thought Clemente, priest or not, had already pulled off a major miracle without so much as opening his mouth, on his first day in the church of San Clemente de Quintás.

"Thank you, sir. What is your name?" were the first words Clemente said, as he looked directly at Ambrosio.

"Ambrosio – you can call me Brosio – at your service."

"And you, ma'am?" he asked, looking at the third bench.

"Domiciana, but you can call me Ladomi like everybody else, or just plain Domi. And, sure, I'm at your service, too," she added, with the familiarity of someone who meant to be on close terms with the new arrival.

"Fine, Domi, Brosio; we'll soon all get to know one another." He looked at the congregation with the easy grace of politicians and rock stars, who stare blindly out into space but manage to seem as though they are looking directly into your eyes, and only yours. The 50 villagers sitting there felt so important in the presence of this new star of their church that, from this moment forth, they all immediately became his devotees – even don Ignacio.

"So happy to be here and greet you all. I am Clemente; I am fascinated by the study of faith and the spirit. I have studied theology for many years; I started at the Salamanca seminary, where I first became a practising priest, though I later acquired more experience in Germany. Now I have recently returned to Spain, and I have been told that you've managed for quite some time here without a parish priest – is that so?" he asked.

"Yes, we've gone without quite a few Masses," said César.

"Well, I suppose I should congratulate you," said Clemente.

"For getting a new priest, or for going without one for so long?" Gaspar asked from the back of the church.

"I see you've got a sense of humour," Clemente answered, "that's good."

"It wouldn't be inappropriate to congratulate us on all these free Sundays we've had," Ambrosio spoke – again!

"The truth is, one can tell how little activity there has been here lately. I have found nothing in the sacristy. We will need some wine and bread if we are going to celebrate the Mass."

"Don't you worry, I'll get it!" said Ignacio from the back. He walked the 50 metres to the bar, and 20 more to find the bread.

He soon returned to the church of San Clemente, and appeared before Clemente with a big loaf of farmer's bread and two short glass tumblers filled with wine.

"Thanks, but one is plenty. This one is for you; drink it, if you like. I only need one," Clemente insisted.

So don Ignacio drank his tumbler, and he felt so astonished by the turn of events he almost came up to give the priest a hug when the point in the Mass came for the parishioners to offer each other the peace.

Mass began, that first Sunday of November, without the hymns to the glory of the Lord that Domi usually led, nor the passing of the collection plate by her friend Maribel. San Clemente de Quintás, a village with 200 citizens in the winter and more than twice that many in the summer months, was beginning, on this fifth of November, a new phase.

CHAPTER IX

Feet on the floor, torso straight, sitting on the edge of the bed. Her body formed the precise outline of the number 4: this meant that she was in San Clemente, sitting on this tall, tall bed. The wood of the floor down there softly caressed her feet, which searched for her slippers with a complex series of movements while her body refused to abandon its seat on the bed.

A wind at her back made her shiver and tremble.

The window pane rattled listlessly inside the wooden frame set in the wall. Aurora couldn't help feeling the chill in the air when she breathed in sharply and looked out at the chestnut trees and the fields of maize in the valley below.

Sometimes a chill can feel cheery when it catches you in your nightgown; it is like the mild shock of mouthwash against your gums: a sweet pain that stings and gives pleasure at the same time.

There was nobody home. And the old house was so fresh and aired-out that it seemed to be smiling at her from every wall. She walked along the corridor and saw the kitchen table laden with green apples and chestnuts. Past them, a plate of her favourite pastries (aniseed-flavoured *rosquillas*) next to the coffee pot and the big mug of hot milk.

The clock said 12.30 – 12.30!

She hadn't heard the rooster crow (she never heard the rooster crow on the first night she slept in her village after returning from Madrid), nor the church bells toll. Her first morning in San Clemente, this 5 November, fell on a Sunday, a day when the rooster crows as he does every day, but when the church bells also ring so loudly that they recall an old, long-standing grudge among villagers.

They say that one Sunday morning, Ambrosio's wife heard a certain old, mean-spirited villager shout himself to death. He had thrown open his window, not far from the windows of Ambrosio and Lidia, and had begun cursing and swearing and hurling abuse at half the village. What he couldn't stand was the noise that the bells made every Sunday morning, and he had even terrorised his closest neighbours with this obsession; he used to say that one day he'd pull out his shotgun.

After that day, Lidia and Ambrosio had woken up feeling tense, Sunday or not. Their neighbour shouted so fiercely, with his eyes so reddened with fury, that he didn't seem human.

One day, the tolling bells completely drowned out his loudest cries; and he, as if possessed by the Devil himself, attacked the bells head-on with his voice, as if he wished to show the bell-ringer that he could outdo them. He shouted louder and louder, and on and on, until he stopped taking the time to breathe. Until one last shout carried him off. He stood speechless at the window.

The bells stopped swinging, but he was already dead. His was a pointless death: the bells of San Clemente had rung out that day as they did every Sunday, yet no one had heard the shouts or the curses that the late Antón had hurled at them. No one but Lidia and Ambrosio, who then fell silent for ever.

They could no longer speak, except in their own home. The man's death had struck them dumb.

And the bells went on ringing, week after week. Maybe they had tolled today as well, but Aurora had been too relaxed to hear them. After her two baths on the balcony the day before, her sleep had been truly restorative.

"What's going on in here?" Aurora asked out loud, as she

leapt around the house. She left no corner of the big old place unturned; this was her way of greeting it. She returned to the balcony and breathed in deeply. She felt she had a good day in front of her.

"Holy shit!" she said, and then she rather coyly covered her lips with her hand, although she was only facing the wooden frame of the wide balcony window. When she was small, her mother Pura had always inspected her lips with a magnifying glass when such foul language had escaped them.

"What are these swear words I'm hearing?" Pura would ask her as soon as she heard her utter some dubious expression. Aurora would scarcely have finished speaking, and there would be her mother, coming over with the magnifying glass in her hand, to inspect her lips, as if to give her a first warning. She had taken that glass out of her purse so many times! Aurora had never caught her without it, not even on that day when they were visiting someone's house and Aurora was running around the courtyard with her little friends. Pura had leaned out the window to show her the magnifying glass, and then gone back to the conversation, as naturally as anything, right where she had left off.

Pura got her point across.

"I've only heard you say *wanker* twice, Aurora, and that's the worst thing you ever say. And anyway, when you say it, it sounds as sweet as the candy floss at a funfair," her friend Fany liked to tell her. And she would say. "You'll never manage to intimidate anybody at that rate, Aurora. Someday I'll have to fly off the handle at you, just to see how you react."

Without swear words, Aurora was woman with a strong personality; yet her mother's persistence won the day, so that – standing here at the age of 30, all by herself in front of the wide balcony window – she still covered her mouth with her hand when she swore at the thought of what a magnificent day it was going to be. From now on, all her days would have to be magnificent.

She got moving.

And so, even without a concrete plan in mind, she felt the need to go down to the village square; so urgent a need that she even passed up the *rosquillas* and the coffee and went straight to the shower. Again she washed her whole body.

She hadn't set foot in the village since summer, and the previous night she had either fallen asleep very early, or her aunt and uncle had come home very late. She hadn't even seen them yet.

"Who'll buy me a coffee?" asked Aurora. She had sneaked up behind her Aunt Domi, who was huddling in Joaquín's bar with a tight circle of villagers not all of whom Aurora recognised.

"Auro! Give us a kiss! And how are you, girl? Here's another one coming in with her hair wet, Father!"

"Please, Domi, don't call me that," said Clemente, whose hair still lay plastered against his scalp in tangled, damp curls.

"Here, Clemente, let me present you to my niece, Aurora."

Something had happened in her niece's life during the three months that had passed since summer. Her aunt noted it straight away: something like flashes of joy flittered across her face. "At last," thought Domi, though there was actually no news in her niece's life; at least, no tangible news, nothing you could tell somebody about, but . . . Aurora was on her way.

After steaming herself for so long in hot water the night before, her skin was almost transparent. The ruddiness in her cheeks came from her jog from the old family house to Joaquín's bar. Her hair was almost dripping on her shoulders; not a trace of her fringe. Not a drop of make-up. With her hair combed back, she was even more beautiful.

"Delighted to meet you," said Aurora to Clemente. She truly was delighted, and this lent her face even more brilliance.

"So you fell into the river, too, Auro?" asked César, lightly pinching the nape of his niece's neck by way of greeting.

She had no idea what he was talking about, but everybody

else laughed, and for today, that was good enough for her. Cradling her coffee cup in her hands, she realised that, indeed, she wasn't the only one in the circle who was dripping wet, but she decided not to ask.

She also realised that she felt at home.

"I can't wait to take a walk around the village!" Aurora blurted out.

"We were just about to give Clemente the tour. He just got here – straight from Germany, no less, just imagine," said César.

"How long will you be staying?" asked Joaquín, from the other side of the bar.

"Couldn't say. I was going to come for a week, but I haven't reached an agreement with the people in the agency, so I just left it open," Aurora stated, with absolute assurance in her left hand (always her most expressive one) and an aniseed-flavoured *rosquilla* in her right (always her most active).

"You don't know how long you'll stick around here, then?" Joaquín persisted, as he began serving them a second round of coffees.

Aurora laughed out loud when she heard Clemente's ironic commentary:

"They warned me about you Galicians: the first thing you ask somebody when he arrives is when he's going to leave or how long he plans to stay."

Joaquín stood there, holding the coffee pot, with a blank look on his face. The others couldn't make it out at all; but Aurora just kept on laughing.

"It's part of our character. It's just a way of showing our hospitality, like any other," she responded.

"It's just that we don't want her to leave," Joaquín added from behind the counter. The blush on his cheeks reminded everyone of his unrequited love.

Before they could move on from coffee to grape juice and from grape juice to wine, which was the usual order of business in Joaquín's bar of a Sunday, César reminded everyone present that their stroll around the village was pending, and that it was time to allow Clemente to get to know the place.

They all set off, and when they reached the school buildings, those who were walking in front came to a halt. Clemente was engrossed in his conversation with Aurora, but he became aware that the pace of the stroll had slowed down, and he looked up and understood: "This must be where I'm going to be living for now. The old teacher's quarters, from the looks of it."

"Yes. My mother used to work here."

"Was she the teacher back then? I met the new teacher yesterday; he just arrived here, too. I think he's from Valencia."

"There are so many new faces in the village . . ." Aurora said evasively.

She didn't tell Clemente that her mother had never become the village teacher, because then she would have had to tell him, in all honesty, that her mother could have filled the job, but that she had become the school cook instead, while she was carrying Aurora in her womb, after a fellow her mother had fallen for had wandered into the maize fields one morning.

The maize fields where Aurora was conceived. The maize fields of her village.

Her mother had never left her, from that moment on.

When she was old enough to go to school, Aurora used to see her mother in the dining hall at playtime. Sometimes Aurora even helped her set the tables. She preferred listening to the tales her mother told her to skipping rope in the playground. With her mother, she could talk about addition and subtraction and about the mysteries of language . . . in a different way.

In this way, Pura became her private tutor, and Aurora felt blessed to have her, and sad at what her schoolmates were missing at playtime.

Her mother soon had a chance to become an art teacher. Aurora didn't feel any prouder of her then; she was proud enough as it was. But now, looking at the fields surrounding the school buildings, she could see her mother setting up a backcloth in front of a tree, several stainless steel pans, an old lamp, and a tin lantern . . . Very curious, the still lifes that the art teacher of the school of San Clemente de Quintás used to arrange.

Another day, she brought Aurora's grandmother as a model. Ignacia made a special effort to put her hair up in a bun that day, and to dress in her best clothes, so confident was she that her daughter's students would have made great strides.

But neither Aurora nor any of her schoolmates could reproduce her grandmother's kindly face. She could have been any grandmother, to tell the truth.

"Well, that's all right, boys and girls. I don't know what your teacher will say, but if anybody else tells you that I don't look like your portraits of me, you should defend your art. Painting is an interpretation of reality, and you are the one and only owners of your own drawings," Ignacia commented.

What she didn't tell them was that she had spent more than an hour getting dressed and made up, just in case some budding genius might manage to capture a jovial and well-dressed woman on a piece of Bristol board.

The eight villagers who were showing Clemente around entered his house. They wanted to see for themselves that his living quarters were in acceptable condition, after a restoration that hardly any of those present had witnessed.

The house looked small now to Aurora – very small. And for good reason: the old teacher's quarters had been divided into two apartments, one for Clemente and the other for Fran, the new school teacher. It was as if the house had multiplied, but the mirage short-changed the old house by several square metres.

The villagers who had set off on the tour half an hour earlier could now see both apartments occupied. Fran was also there, unpacking his bags and placing books on shelves.

"Hello, good afternoon," Fran said to the group, without looking at anyone in particular. Aurora caught sight of a pale, almost feverish face that looked completely lost.

They continued on to Clemente's house, which was filled with unopened packages. Still empty, the rooms were waiting to come to life. A laptop computer drew Aurora's attention: it was the same shade of blue as the Galician sky on a sunny day.

"What a lovely colour," she said in a low voice. If she had felt more at home, she would have asked him to let her see it. The group had already moved into the kitchen when Clemente turned back and found her, staring at his laptop.

"Do you like computing?" he asked.

"It is a necessity," Aurora said in a laconic tone, with a kind of formality that was out of character for her. "The truth is, I've only used a computer to type up my c.v. for a recruitment agency."

"If you need it, borrow it. These laptops are just like the big ones, they work the same."

"Your password could be *clemente*, just like that. It has eight characters already."

"You've guessed it."

Clemente stayed on in his house, talking to his new neighbour. The others went home to their own houses, since it was nearing three in the afternoon – time for dinner and a nap. The fog was rolling in while the people, on their way home, talked about how best to split up all the tasks to be done in preparation for the feast day of San Martín, 11 November. They agreed to meet and discuss it that afternoon in Joaquín's bar.

Aurora knew she wouldn't be going back out.

Fog always seems thicker on a Sunday; and if it is November, too, everything grows as dark as the mouth of a hayloft. They reached the imposing entrance to the house, and the distant barking of a dog filled Aurora with a sudden impulse to shut the door and run upstairs, so that she could enjoy the sight of the village from the window.

"Do you still keep a brazier under the warming table?" asked Aurora.

"Of course I do!" her aunt replied cheerily. The truth was, she really wanted to have a talk with her niece.

There was leftover braised beef with potatoes. "Galician potatoes," as Aurora called them when she was still readjusting to her home town. She also called them this when she was back in Madrid and bringing them to mind. But after a while back in San Clemente de Quintás, they became just potatoes, pure and simple.

And in front of the potatoes, two asparagus stalks were marking the time, as if the plate were imitating a clock and the stalks of wild asparagus, its hands.

In any case, it was half-past three in the afternoon. Dinnertime.

CHAPTER X

On her fifth day in San Clemente de Quintás, Aurora's friend Fany called again. Everything was so unsettled on the eve of San Martín's day, the great night of the *Magosto* in her village, that she was ready to hear anything without being shocked.

"Hi, what's up?" Aurora asked, without much interest.

"Nothing, just that I said no to the beauty parlour. It would have been for only three and a half months, and then what?"

"But isn't that what you studied to do? So, it must be something you like doing. You could go on finding your own way after that job."

"What difference does it make, Aurora? They've moved me up to checkout counter two, it's not as cold there, I received my first pay cheque, and I don't have an end date for my job," Fany replied, with pure, disillusioned conviction. "In any case, they have my name on file now, with all my particulars," she went on, "and that's always good."

"What's the name for the spot at the back of the knee, the one you had such trouble memorising, remember? For that beautician's exam? The . . ."

"The popliteal cavity," she replied effortlessly and with an utter lack of enthusiasm.

"What a massage you gave me one day, between my calf and the back of my knee," Aurora reminded her. She was unable to stir the slightest bit of nostalgia; Fany had decided that she wasn't moving from the Mediodía supermarket.

A brief silence.

"Well, I'm happy for you. Let the *Talento* agency find somebody else," Aurora said with disdain, though at heart she was hoping that Fany would tell her how the interview had gone. She didn't know if Fany had mentioned her.

"Auro . . ." It was the first time her neighbour had called her by that name. "You have to go to the temp agency. They think you're crazy."

"What?"

"I said, they think you're crazy. Well, maybe it's a bit extreme to put it that way . . . The thing is, they don't go in for letters there. Everything is much more practical. They showed me all the letters you've written them, and they told me they don't know what to do. They don't take you seriously. From what they read to me, you told them a lot about me – about the Fnac prize; how I'm a responsible person because I've never skipped work even when I was under the weather . . . They thought that was funny, but it was what made them decide to interview me, or so they told me, and so, thanks . . . They read me your letters at the interview. It left me a little speechless, Aurora; you know, you tell them everything . . ."

"Well, I can see how much good that's done for you," said Aurora, steaming with anger.

"No, Aurora – I got them to make an appointment for you with the psychologist. I mean, he wants to see you."

"Well, thanks a lot – that's all I need!"

"It isn't what you think. The psychologists are the ones who decide who gets the jobs. The one who wants to see you is a guy named Guillermo. I don't know him, but they gave me his card and they told me you should call him to make an appointment. His name is . . ." Fany looked at the small white card, traced with fine blue letters. "Guillermo Fernández Casa. Write down his phone number. 91 . . ."

"Well, thanks," Aurora side-stepped the issue after lack-adaisically jotting down the number on the first page of a magazine she had at hand.

"How're things up there?" Fany asked her, surprised by Aurora's muted response to the good news she had delivered. Faced with this calm, yet somehow surly reaction, Fany couldn't decide how to keep going with the conversation, but she needed to keep it up because she still hadn't finished. There was something she needed to ask of Aurora, and it was a rather ticklish subject.

"Fine, just fine. The fiesta is tomorrow, and everything's in an uproar. And when there's a moment to spare, I even do some crochet work, sitting at the warming table in the living room."

"How's that?"

"Like I said. I do a little of everything. Here, I get up nice and early, and I get lots done every day, I really do. I've borrowed a laptop from someone, and it even has a CD drive and speakers for listening to music. Last night I discovered Bach's *Mass in B Minor*. They let me borrow a whole pile of CDs, and I can listen to them at the computer," Aurora said enthusiastically. Fany seized upon her improved mood.

"Auro . . .," (the second time she had called her by that name). "Could you lend me the keys to your flat? Well, that is, I already have them, what I mean is that . . . I wanted to ask you if . . . if you minded if I used them, if I could go up there with Tomás."

Another brief silence, though it seemed endless to Fany.

For 30 seconds, a complete inventory of her household danced through Aurora's mind. The images seemed to move in black and white to the beat of a distant, barely audible waltz. Everything danced in her mind: her towels, her Portuguese sheets, her feather pillows, the kitchen gadgets, the upholstery of her favourite easy chair in front of the television, the flowerpots on the balcony, the bath soap . . . She could see Roberto among the feathers, among the bath bubbles, in the bath, in the bed, in her arms, frying up eggs, wearing the red-striped apron that was still perfectly usable and hung behind the kitchen door . . .

She still hadn't answered. It was a difficult request, and both of them knew it.

. . . Spoons, knives, tin openers, forks . . . A few things in her flat did not brim with life, but these! Before Aurora's mind there appeared the diminutive linen napkins, the ones that were still waiting for a special occasion, in the second drawer of the sideboard.

The linen lay next to the china – just a few big, white plates. Nuclear white, the whitest white, as the ads say on television.

Fragile and strong at the same time, like the moon; that's what Roberto used to say.

Actually, as they lay next to the yellowing linen, these plates were still intact and alive. Full moons, waiting in the sideboard . . . These four nuclear plates conserved the memory of the aurora borealis in their gleaming surfaces, and that made it somehow easier for Aurora to give her friend the answer she was waiting for.

"Fany, please take good care of my things. Rather, leave them alone, leave them all, don't touch anything," said Aurora, still a bit lost in her daydreams.

. . . There was going to be a full moon tomorrow, San Martín's day. It was already clearly visible in the greyish-blue sky of these last evening hours. It seemed impossible for this moon to get any fatter than it was – like when you blow up a balloon and you think, enough, that's it, no way you can inflate it any more . . .

If words were forks, they wouldn't be able to punch a hole in the moon in this evening's sky, it could never be deflated, because it was hard as a porcelain plate. Nonetheless, Aurora and Roberto – in complete accord even without seeing each other – allowed it to shatter, as if a piece of china had been dropped from a great height to the ground. The moon, filled with memories, was smashed to pieces like a damaged plate, and the tiny sparkling lights in the sky were no other than the end and the beginning of everything. Life in movement.

"Don't touch anything, OK, Fany?" she said once more.

"Thanks. We'll talk, we'll talk soon. Bye, love."

And the checkout operator finally hung up the phone with these few words. She took two long strides down the corridor of her flat until she reached the kitchen. She quickly downed a chicken breast and a banana, and ran up the stairs. Half an hour still remained before the Mediodía supermarket reopened its doors for the afternoon, and, as was beginning to be the norm, her workmate was waiting for her in the bed on the fifth floor.

CHAPTER XI

13 November 2000

To: Guillermo Fernández Casa
From: Aurora Ortiz Menéndez

You can start laughing now, you and all your colleagues at the agency; please, keep right on chortling at me and at all the things I've been telling you. I'm sure you've missed my letters lately, since, after all, without these distractions, life in your office must be very boring.

So please, go and tell your colleagues that Aurora Ortiz, the aspiring caretaker, is back.

I've come back to say goodbye; for, after all, even if one hasn't studied at university, one can act educated.

Believe me, I was beginning to realise that I was perhaps telling you too many stories that led in the wrong direction in my most recent letters. But why did I let myself chop my life into little bits, so that you could read them like the ruthlessly honest chapters of a bewildered woman's story?

I simply did it because it was the only way I knew how to speak about myself and my qualifications for a possible job, which I desire more than anything else in the world.

If I was going about it the wrong way, why couldn't

you have found some other way to let me know? You never answered my letters.

Why have I kept writing to you, time and time again? My mother succeeded many times through her sheer persistence; I inherited her tenacity but not her results. She even managed to get me to keep from saying everything that went through my mind, got me to restrain my words, but in these past weeks I haven't even managed to make the cut and be called to an interview. Not even if I had sent you 80 letters.

My mother restrained my words, but nobody could stop my thoughts.

You can imagine the words it would take to express how much I loathe you. Fany, whom you know very well, has told me that you consider me crazy; and you are quite right: I must be daft not to report you for your heartlessness and unprofessionalism.

Aurora Ortiz Menéndez

*

This time when she dropped the letter in the box, she was full of conviction. She went all the way to the village square of Lonxo, a larger village with a better infrastructure than San Clemente de Quintás, just three kilometres away. She even asked Ignacio the tobacconist to give her a first-class stamp, so that her letter would get to where it was going in Madrid as soon as possible.

She walked to Lonxo, preferring her own leg power to her Uncle César's car. The eucalyptus trees kept her company all the way there. She had always liked that tree; biologists say that it destroys the land wherever it sprouts, but there must be something wrong with that way of thinking, because all the woods around her village were full of life, and full of eucalyptus.

The only bad thing about that kind of tree, her grandfather once told her, is that when a really heavy rainstorm hits, it doesn't provide enough shelter. Eucalyptus trees are like enormously tall umbrellas that are full of holes. Aurora recalled her grandfather's words as she looked up, higher and higher, into the sky.

And suddenly, rain was more than just a threatening thought.

She picked up the pace, pulling on a hood, striding with her boots – like fishing boots, but lower and more comfortable. She wasn't bothered; as the rain filtered down through the eucalyptus, it seemed to her like a nutritious sap, or like one of nature's practical jokes, as if someone were clapping his hands under a gigantic tap above her head.

Someday she would figure out the reason for all this applause.

A car – not very new, but fairly powerful – pulled up abruptly and stopped. The right-hand window went down at the push of a button; Aurora gave a friendly yet distant greeting to the man at the wheel, since she wasn't entirely sure who he was. After she had got into the car, she remembered his name. It was Fran, the new school teacher.

He had already asked his neighbour, Clemente, about Aurora.

"Thanks for the lift. I'm soaked; the thing is, even though I'm a Galician myself, I've never been a big fan of umbrellas. They isolate you from the environment, in front, behind, on all sides . . . everywhere," she said, smiling as she said these last words, so that her eyes met Fran's just as they hit the middle of a poorly asphalted curve.

"Oh, dear, pardon me. I'm still not used to the roads around here," Fran said, correcting the steering wheel.

Fortunately, no one was heading towards them.

"What brings you here?"

"Well, San Clemente is my village, and Lonxo is my municipality," Aurora replied sarcastically. "I just went to post a letter," she added, to soften the irony.

"But the post is collected in San Clemente, isn't it?"

"Oh, but it is so much slower."

"I just went to buy some materials that we need for the school. If I'd had any idea you were also going to Lonxo, I would have given you a lift. It wouldn't have cost me anything," said Fran, knowing that it was a short ride and that he would have to make the best use of it.

"Thanks, very kind of you." It would have been cruel of her to say that she loved taking walks by herself.

His face looked more pleasant than she remembered from the first time she'd seen him, on the walking tour of the village with Clemente. Aurora recalled him surrounded by packages, still unpacking his bags, and looking quite pale. Even now, his skin could hardly be described as rosy; it had a whitish tinge, like the hue of the whitewash that is splattered on houses in the south of Spain.

She hadn't seen him again since that day. Not even up on Monte Fariña during the *Magosto*. The new school teacher had been all set to go, but in the end he had decided that he'd rather stay at home; the thought of having to greet all the kids and their parents rather weighed him down. That night, he hadn't been in the mood for socialising, so he had knocked on his neighbour's door and told Clemente that he wasn't feeling well.

But now, at this moment, he found it quite pleasant to answer every question asked by this woman in the passenger seat of his car. Aurora felt her innate curiosity taking off; when that curiosity came upon her, as it did now, there was no way to slow it down. That was why, after they had left the car parked in the village square, it was inevitable that she would continue her interrogation in Joaquín's bar.

It was between opening the door to the bar and sitting down in front of a couple of glasses of wine that Aurora discovered he was not from Valencia, as everyone in the village supposed, but from further south, in Murcia, though he had gone to Santiago de Compostela in Galicia to study. It had pained him to have to leave that city for San Clemente – a tiny, faraway village that he could barely find on a map; yet two years here would give him more points toward a promotion than any town closer to Santiago. And besides, this was where the lottery had assigned him, so it was unavoidable.

"And where would you rather be?"

"In the navy, no question."

"What?"

"Oh, you mean, as a teacher? I hadn't understood you. Well, I'd prefer Santiago, of course, but that would be difficult."

Deep in her heart, it angered Aurora that this man, sitting here at the table with her, sharing a wine from the region, should hold her village, and no doubt her village school, in greater disdain than he dared admit; perhaps that was why Fran hadn't even bothered to go up to the fiesta on Monte Fariña the night of San Martín. These villages in the interior of Galicia, so far from the sea, held little attraction for him; so he sought refuge each night in the light of the reading lamp in his room. Some nights, the reading lamp; other nights, he would also surf the Internet to meet up with his friends from Santiago, all scattered now across Galicia; they would send each other loquacious emails and funny images, which he was reproducing now in words for Aurora.

He spoke of the Internet with pleasure. It completely transformed his face.

"Yes, I handle computers, too; I had one in Madrid, and now Clemente has left me his for the few days I'm here," Aurora said with just the right amount of interest, turning to gaze out the window. Her apparent disregard was appreciated not so much by Fran as by Joaquín, who hadn't taken his eyes off her since she entered the bar.

"Don't you like it when they send you things? Don't tell me you don't have email, or use chat rooms," Fran rebuked her, forcefully exhaling a puff of cigarette smoke.

"Well . . ." Aurora wasn't sure how to evade the question. Both her computers were on loan, and she had never had an email account. To be perfectly honest, she scarcely knew what he was talking about.

"I prefer having a 'sweet little rap', in the words of my Ecuadorian neighbours in Madrid," she finally declared.

"What's that?" He didn't quite understand.

"A 'sweet little rap' is . . . a good chat. We've often spent hours chatting without realising it; we might start off talking about volcanoes, and end up, who knows – it's impossible to predict."

"What's Madrid like? Is it true that you have to queue for everything?" Fran was trying to pick a good topic.

"I don't know . . . Nobody's ever asked me that."

At that moment she knew for certain that this man – though he was her own age; though she had shared a car, a table, and a bottle of wine with him; for all that he had come from a big city and had been born in a city facing the sea – had such a lifeless sneer that even her little village would be too big for him.

She didn't want to be too cruel in her thoughts, but in this instant she understood clearly that Fran would not have an easy time of it in San Clemente. We all deserve a second chance, she told herself; maybe I'm misinterpreting him, she insisted to herself; but in the end, she looked at Roberto's watch (still on her right wrist) and exclaimed how late it was: really, she had to be going.

She didn't even ask him why he hadn't joined the navy.

Fran saw her to the big front door of her house, and there they ran into Clemente. Aurora had forgot her Aunt Domi's invitation to him on San Martín's night, when they were sharing sticks to roast sausages over the bonfire on Monte Fariña. And chestnuts, too. A snack for supper, that was it. She had forgotten. Fran didn't have a chance to invite Aurora to do anything else, so he said, "Well, if you're ever headed back to Lonxo, don't hesitate to call on me."

The sheer absurdity of these words struck him like a lightning bolt as soon as he turned away from Clemente and Aurora, who were already closing the door and turning to climb the stairs.

It was at this moment, when Fran was heading back to the square for his car and Domi was greeting the newcomers, that some of the neighbours who were watching this situation murmured out loud their doubts about Clemente – whether he was really a priest, or whether he was a suitor.

"Here you are, both with wet hair again!" Domi observed as she greeted them from the kitchen, a wooden spoon in her hand. They looked at each other: they hadn't even noticed.

CHAPTER XII

Stuffbread. *Pan preñao*. This dish was the centrepiece of the evening; Clemente wanted to find out what a loaf of farmer's bread tasted like when it had been hollowed out and filled with a selection of melted cheeses that Domi had bought in Ourense. Not local cheeses; cheeses from all over the world: Parmesan, Emmental . . . all accompanied by a touch of white wine and a dash of olive oil.

Good, locally bottled wines and homemade meatballs rounded out the informal supper, which ended with the finishing touch of pears from their own orchard, and an almond tart, which Clemente himself had brought over, protecting it from the rain as best he could.

"What a delightful table, and delightful table mates!" Clemente exclaimed contentedly, looking at the others sitting around the massive chestnut table that had been carved by Domi's husband several years earlier from a single block of wood. This table, covered by a cloth and the groaning plates, had won him over simply by its feeling of solidity and its four sturdy legs.

"Would you like to bless the table, Clemente?" Domi asked the guest.

He turned to face the loaf of bread (as if looking for the right words), and then lowered his eyes to his plate. The others kept their eyes on him.

"Oh Lord our God, thank you for being here, with Domi, César, Mercedes and Aurora. Thank you for the hospitality of these new friends and their good deeds. Help us, Lord, to know how to help those who have less than us, now that we are about to break this . . . What's the name for it, Domi?" Clemente asked, raising his eyes slightly.

"Stuffbread, that's what we call it," Domi said with obvious embarrassment, prompting a sidelong smile from her friend Mercedes.

"Now that we break, oh Lord our God, this *stuffbread*, which Domi has so lovingly made for us. Amen," Clemente concluded, lifting his eyes from the plate.

"Amen," the others added, feeling a bit awkward.

Good thing Mercedes was there, too – one of those ignorant people who don't have an ounce of malice in them, as Domi had secretly described her to Aurora when her friend had gone overboard in her choice of words to describe her niece's mother. Her lack of reflection did not cancel out her other qualities, however, such as loyalty, honesty and an unlimited willingness to give of herself when times were tough.

She was truly Domi's best friend. César called them "Domi and her indomitable friend" when the pair went out of an afternoon to enjoy fried bread and hot chocolate.

Besides, people who have no sense of shame can sometimes get you out of a difficult situation.

"I'm dying to see your face when you try the stuffbread, Señor Clemente," said Mercedes as she spread her napkin elegantly across her lap.

"Please, just call me Clemente. When will I manage to convince you?" the new priest asked in a relaxed tone, rolling up his sleeves.

It wasn't the first time they had shared a meal, nor wine and liqueurs. On San Martín's night, this group and others had leapt over the embers of the bonfire as if it had been Midsummer's Night. Clemente, who was from the neighbouring province of

Asturias, learned many Galician songs that night. Some he had already known.

"Galicians and Asturians – first cousins, eh, Padre?" many villagers, especially the older ones, told him on the Monte that night.

Clemente worked hard to get past being the village novelty. Nonetheless, his youthful spirit set him so far apart from his predecessor in the parish that his popularity, by contrast, grew day by day.

He comforted the sick with the same strength of character with which he read the children's poems of Gloria Fuertes out loud to the kids at school; he jogged through the meadows in shorts, whatever the weather; he stopped to watch the cows graze and the bees make their journeys from flower to hive. He prepared his Sunday sermons with the help of a committee of villagers, for two reasons, as he explained: first, this way he didn't feel alone; second, he wanted to hear questions from those who, up to now, had only faced the pulpit and listened. One of the first of these committees was headed by Ambrosio.

"Questions make the world go round, don't they, Clemente?"

"It wouldn't be a bad thing if they did. If we could just get this village to change a little, we could be happy . . ."

During their trimester on the committee, Ambrosio and his group set the stage for beginning the restoration of the sacristy; they also organised a roster for putting a freshly cut flower before the image of San Martín each day, just as they did before the images of the Virgin Mary and other saints. They decided to propose to the rest of the parishioners the idea of not passing the collection plate during Mass, but instead, of asking each churchgoer to place a donation in the box at the entrance to the church whenever he or she wished. They also decided that everyone should donate a coin before lighting one of the small candles for an offering, but only until they had collected enough money to buy a new Bible. Then they would set aside this custom of giving money for the right to light a tiny candle with a match and pray. If their calculations were correct, this service should be paid off by approximately next summer. Then prayer would be free.

Their proposals made a good package.

The committee members who followed took up where the first ones had left off. Because of their proposals, parishioners began to express improvised prayers of thanksgiving and of supplication during the Mass; they learned new hymns; and César was put in charge of finding the tools and the manpower to restore the back door to the church building, if they could safely open a breach in what had become a supporting wall for the whole church.

Attendance was going up. Whether or not they felt a sense of peace when they left the Romanesque church of San Clemente, the congregation kept on huddling in the village square afterwards, or heading to one house or another for intense conversations if the weather didn't permit them to stay outside.

A few months later, the members of the third committee raised a few questions of a much more ambitious scope. Questions about riches and repentance, and also about the Church, which . . .

". . . Which is one, but isn't one. I don't know if you understand what I'm getting at," Gaspar had asked obliquely. "I read something about it in *La Región,* but I wouldn't be able to reproduce it now," he went on, leaving his half-formed quotation hanging in mid-air. "There's the Protestants, there's us, the Catholics, there's the Anglicans . . . But shouldn't it all be the same, Clemente?" he asked again.

"Just stop bothering everybody else and stop talking nonsense, and you'll be saved," said Ignacio the tobacconist.

"That doesn't seem sufficient," Clemente said.

"Well, for me, times being what they are, if nobody pesters me, I consider myself happy."

"I think this business of all the religions is like a big octopus: one good head and lots of tentacles. What difference does it make if it's one tentacle or the other? Some of us are over here, others over there – the main thing is the head of the octopus," argued Fina, the veterinarian's widow.

Clemente was enjoying his time with them more and more.

That day they ended up talking about pentagrams.

"Music unites people from all over, it doesn't pay any attention to different religions," Clemente said, introducing a new idea.

He realised that, apart from the bands that had played during the summer fiestas, they had heard little music in the village. Clemente had fallen in love with Bach during his stay in Germany; he offered to lend his CDs out, on the condition that they followed the lyrics that were printed in the little CD booklet.

Some of them listened to the *Passion According to Saint Matthew*, others heard the *Cantatas*, others the *Christmas Oratorio* as interpreted by a Japanese orchestra, others the *Passion According to Saint John* . . . It was a big shock at first, but by reading the lyrics, just as Clemente had asked them to, they all came to feel that they had been spending a few marvellous hours singing the Lord's praise.

They went to the next planned meeting of the third committee with a certain sense of quiet reflectiveness. Clemente put his question forward as soon as the meeting began.

"Was Bach a man of faith?"

"No doubt about it," everyone answered in unison.

"And do you think he practised his faith?"

"How should we know? We weren't around back then!" said Ignacio, and they all laughed.

"I believe he must have done. His music is one big prayer."

"And that prayer, that belief: is it Catholic, for instance, or Protestant?" Clemente asked.

There was a long silence.

"I'm thinking about that octopus again . . . I don't know, it's all the same to me," Fina said.

"Who listened to the *Mass in B Minor*?"

"I did," said Gaspar.

"Who listened to the *Christmas Oratorio*?" Clemente asked.

"We did," said Domi and César, "and then we passed it along to Joaquín, but he couldn't come today."

"What can you tell us about it?"

"I dunno – it moved us," replied César.

"Bach was a Protestant. A Lutheran, to be precise," the new priest informed them.

He thought they all seemed somehow disappointed.

"Does that really make a difference?" he asked them. "Of all his works, only one, the *Mass in B Minor*, is Catholic. And why was that one? Because it was commissioned by Augustus III, who was none other than the father-in-law of our own Charles III: a German who converted to Catholicism when he was elected King of Poland.

"In any case," he went on, "there are many who insist that it is a Protestant Mass, because it has so much choral music, which is a common trait of Protestant religious services . . . It is . . . It is a singular work, whose roots lie in the world of enigma.

"Enigma, what a great word, eh?" He looked around the room.

"I see the High Mass as an act of reconciliation among the different branches of the faith; but more than that, it is a reconciliation with history, with changing styles, with tradition. Even with the future . . .

"This Mass, which some of us have been able to hear . . .," he said, in an attempt to reopen the discussion.

"Yes, we'll have to start trading the CDs with each other," Domi broke in.

"Of course," said Clemente. "As I was saying," he went on, "Bach completed the *Mass in B Minor*, which some of us have heard, during his lifetime, but he never got to hear it performed himself." Clemente sat in pensive silence for a moment. "How I would love to know why Bach put such effort into writing something he knew he would never hear! That shows true human mastery . . .

"And there are people who still debate, more than three centuries after his birth, whether this work is a Catholic or a Protestant Mass."

"Maybe the beautiful thing about it is that we'll never know," said Ambrosio.

"That's what I think, too, Ambrosio," Clemente said. "But let's keep talking."

There was no doubt that Clemente had won the respect of all his friends and parishioners. Nor was there any question about his commitment and his rectitude, the righteousness of his spirit, or the clarity of his intentions.

But these conversations came much later, a few days before the first anniversary of the moment he first set foot on the soil of this village in the back country of Ourense – a soil that turned slippery on the banks of the river, and which had inevitably made him fall into the water when he tried to calm his nerves a few minutes before saying his first Mass in San Clemente de Quintás.

Back then, within days of his arrival, he had already enjoyed Domi's stuffbread, and the wagging tongues of the village were busy discussing his feelings for Aurora and, much more than that, the question of whether or not he really was a priest. Some went so far as to propose an investigation of how he had got here, to this village that held 200 people in the winter and that was accustomed to being caught up in every manner of dodge and swindle.

Clemente soon revealed his true character: he had never fooled anyone.

Nor did he want to fool himself.

Supper ended, and on to dessert. After the stuffbread, the homemade meatballs, the pears fresh from the orchard, and the almond tart. After the coffee and the cherry-flavoured liqueur; after explaining to Aurora how to connect to the Internet with his laptop – after all that, Clemente and Aurora sat together on the balcony for the first time, united by a single conversation and a single language.

In Aurora, he discovered the perfect companion. She, the constant questioner, was now the one who had to listen. He told her that he was the one who had asked to be sent to San Clemente, because it was the most isolated place that he could find. He confessed that he had set aside his time in San Clemente for reflection, though at the same time his enthusiasm would make him move mountains if it were necessary in order to help others in the exercise of their faith.

"Sometimes, when I think about my life in the priesthood, I see it as a job, but I really shouldn't look at it that way," he said regretfully. "When I was at the seminary in Salamanca, I was the happiest man alive. After that, two years in Germany opened my eyes. When you go beyond your own borders, you also broaden your outlook. But nothing made me doubt myself. I plunged into the priesthood with the greatest affection . . . Because, if you really want to know something, you have to feel affection for it. Antipathy will never let you get to know it as well." Clemente smiled for the first time.

"Well, you don't look like you've been struggling with your job," said Aurora. "Just look at how everybody treats you – I've never seen the church like this."

"How would you know, if you never go to Mass? And could I ask you why you don't?" asked Clemente.

"My mother has a spot reserved for me in Heaven. I'm sure she's put her bag down so that nobody else will sit next to her!" said Aurora.

"Come on . . ."

After a silence that allowed them to listen to the crickets chirping in the garden, Clemente told Aurora about his tireless energy.

He said, with great caution so as not to hurt himself with

his words, that he often thought his energy was an extraordinary force, which he should share with others: the essence of his faith, the path of his priesthood. At other times, however, he believed that his vitality could never be exhausted; not even if he were put in charge of three parishes could he suppress the anguish that grew inside him from feeling the excess of unlived force, which accumulated day by day, like small doses of cortisone.

"I've always been so anarchic! It's so hard for me not to question everything I see; it's hard for me to obey superiors when they don't deign to speak . . . I've had so many disappointments . . ."

"Clemente, you ask for a lot; that's why you'll be able to change so many things, here and beyond." That was all Aurora could find to say to him.

Clemente left that night without knowing where he was or where he wanted to be. What he did do was to ask Aurora to wait a while longer; not to leave the village just yet.

"Wait until my birthday, at least, on the 23rd," Clemente asked her. "There aren't many people in the village with whom I can speak like this."

"That's fine. I'm in no hurry; I've left the agency that I was using."

"Wouldn't it be better to see that psychologist at the agency who expressed an interest in you?" Clemente asked. "Your Aunt Domi told me all about it, and I think you may have been too hasty."

Domi and Clemente often talked about Aurora.

When he talked with Domi, he learned about her past, from the days when she was called Aurorita and always put her shoes on the wrong feet, up to when her husband died in Madrid.

When he talked with Aurora, on the other hand, they discussed serious issues, and planned her transition to the world of work. Beyond that, their conversations could take them in any direction, and in spite of the fact that they were getting to know each other very well, each of them was constantly being surprised. They were travelling together through the desert of restlessness and temperament, as Clemente once told her when they were strolling near the river.

The village gossip grew – it was noted how often they were seen together, here and there, so wrapped up in their words – and even in their gazes, some began to claim.

They became friends for life.

CHAPTER XIII

After the fiestas of San Martín, the few streets that made up the village returned to normal. To tell the truth, not much was moving on those streets during the last days of November. Snowfall made it hard to take a stroll anywhere near the river once evening fell, and evening was falling a bit earlier every day.

Two weeks in San Clemente already; there wasn't a single line Aurora hadn't read in either of the two books she had picked out for the trip. She had thought she would finish them in a week, going at her usual pace; in the end, she spent two weeks with them, a fortnight in all.

Aurora found the tranquillity she sought through crocheting rugs, listening to CDs, surfing the Internet, and attempting to order her thoughts by setting them down on her borrowed laptop computer. She also found calm in clearing out the wardrobes, getting rid of the outdated clothes that her Aunt Domi still stored in them.

And she spent hours each day talking to Clemente.

They learned so much about their lives and about the lives of their souls that, for the first time, Aurora wished she'd had more time to discover the spiritual mysteries of Roberto. She recalled his face. It was an image of goodness personified; his workmates at Renfe still sent her a lottery ticket every Christmas – that was how much they missed him.

It was the first time she thought about Roberto in isolation, rather than in terms of the world through which he'd moved. She often spoke with other people about Roberto, she still needed him, but, during this trip to San Clemente, her village offered her a new perspective. She no longer saw Roberto romping through the maize fields, or picking almonds, or arguing with Joaquín in the bar in defence of the Vigo Celtas; she didn't even imagine him sitting down with his cup of coffee and his *roscos de vino* at the warming table in her aunt and uncle's house, the same house where she was staying now, the same warming table on which she was resting her elbows while reading the back page of *La Región*.

This time, she didn't even call her inlaws in Vigo to send them her regards on the anniversary. It had been three years.

She was grateful that Roberto hadn't been buried nearby, in the municipal cemetery of Lonxo. Every visit would have meant heartache; she preferred to keep him alive in her memory, and his remains somewhere else, drifting through the atmosphere.

With his family's permission, Aurora had gone to the Casa de Campo park in Madrid. She had set the alarm clock for an earlier hour than she had ever dreamed of waking, except the time they had gone on their honeymoon and got up at four in the morning to avoid the traffic leaving Madrid. And now, on this occasion, she set it once more for four in the morning.

Gingerly carrying the urn containing his ashes, Aurora hailed a taxi to take her to the lake in Casa de Campo. The driver looked at her in his rear-view mirror with some surprise.

"Just let me know where you want me to drop you off," the cabby asked her, avoiding her eye, when they had entered the fenced park and driven a couple of kilometres.

"Right here is fine," Aurora replied, looking out the window.

The lake was calm; the boats were tied up on the shore, and the water was still, so still that it didn't seem the right spot to scatter Roberto's ashes: they would float listlessly away, like dry parsley on top of a stew, and she didn't want to stand there impassively, watching such a slow spectacle.

She walked on, but kept encountering black prostitutes, no matter which way she turned. They became her guides, because, in avoiding them, she discovered that they were pointing her towards an oasis of peace. She climbed over a fence, then stopped to rest against a tree, and there she recited a strange prayer that her grandmother Ignacia had taught her. Her grandmother, like Aurora, had learned it as a girl, and had gone through life without understanding it.

> *Jesus Christ went to Mass with great serenity,*
> *Carrying the Host in the communion cup, full of sanctity.*
> *To one side walked Saint Peter,*
> *To the other side walked Saint John,*
> *And in between the two of them*
> *The twelve apostles came.*
> *All of them ate at one table,*
> *All ate one loaf of bread.*
> *Whoever prays this prayer*
> *Three times before going to bed*
> *Will absolve more of his sins*
> *Than the sea has grains of sand,*
> *And like the blades of grass in the field,*
> *All will be forgiven.*

Aurora had never understood it either, but just in case, she recited the prayer three times. Three times, before going to bed, just as it said. Roberto, all his sins pardoned, went to bed for ever, on a field of grass that was at once familiar and anonymous. He had few sins for which he needed to be forgiven; fortunately, the heart attack had felled one of those people who are ready to board the train at a moment's notice.

Aurora still spoke to him; she recalled how he had pulled the oars on the boat in the lake so near; she told him a thousand times that she loved him; and she wept for the first time since his death. Her strength collapsed at six in the morning, when she let go of Roberto, giving him up to the earth in the same way someone might give breadcrumbs to the birds on a sunny Sunday morning.

It is harder to see tears in the dark. Aurora wasn't fond of weeping; she had been raised to be strong.

"Girl, you haven't even begun to suffer yet," her grandmother Ignacia would tell her when Aurora, as a young child, would recount some unpleasant incident. "You haven't begun to suffer," Ignacia would tell her over and over, while brushing the hair out of her face.

An odd way of comforting her, Aurora thought in her little girl's words, when what she really needed was a more concrete remedy, a solution that was less upsetting, and definitely more hopeful.

She jumped back over the fence, then wandered all over, unable to find her way back. Dawn had not yet broken and her bones were stiff with cold. She suddenly got an urge to leave the empty urn in a rubbish bin that she found as she walked aimlessly; but no, she couldn't abandon it. She didn't think it would be wise to leave a clue for anybody who had a better sense of direction than she – someone who might figure out that the ashes of a fellow man lay nearby.

She stuck the urn in her large bag, and, beginning to worry now, she wiped away her tears once and for all and set out to find the way back to the lake. The Metro was open by this time, and it could take her home to rest.

After tracing long paths and their many branches, like a system of blackened veins; after taking a thousand wrong turns, she cheered up when she saw the women from Central Africa, still in search of business, and knew she was no longer lost.

The prostitutes were drinking hot coffee from a thermos. They even offered her a cup.

"No, thanks; if I have any, I won't be able to sleep."

But she did ask them how to get out of there. Her tears were gone, but the traces of her weeping remained.

She left, and all the women's eyes followed her. They didn't ask her anything, but they gave her something like a hug, without straying from their posts. More and more of the prostitutes appeared as she made her way along the curving paths: motionless, stable, nearby. And full of curves, themselves.

Aurora would never again meet finer examples of respect and anonymous companionship than those offered by the whores in Casa de Campo.

As she sank into her bed to rest, she thought of two new reasons to give in to sweet, tranquil sleep. She would never be able to find the place where she had given her husband back to nature – her hopeless, incorrigible sense of direction would not permit it. And she was almost thankful for this. She wouldn't have to go to one particular spot to feel him near to her.

By coincidence, near the trees where Roberto found his final rest, just beyond the prostitutes from Sierra Leone, there were always cars parked, with couples in them making love.

That was the second reason why she felt comforted.

If Aurora had been able to raise her head up to four times the height of a cypress tree, she would have realised that the line of cars, prudently spaced apart from one another, formed a great circle around Roberto's remains.

Couple without homes to call their own: a genuine honour guard for her love's hideaway.

CHAPTER XIV

"Happy birthday, Clemente," Aurora told him as soon as she was awake enough to call him that November 23. "I have a present for you."

"I've organised a little party at my house this afternoon – could you come early and help me with the cake?" he asked.

By four in the afternoon, Aurora was walking up the path past the school. As soon as he opened the door for her, she gave him a big package wrapped in gift paper.

"Watch out, it's heavy. It's your computer," she said, smiling. "My gift is on it. It's called *aurora.doc*. It's just a few words from me, to say goodbye."

Aurora had cut her hair. She took advantage of having Domi there in the house, and, barely giving her aunt enough time to run and get her haircutting tools, she asked her to cut it as short as she wished. Her aunt couldn't believe it: she had been after Aurora for so many years in the hopes of lightening her thick mane that now, without pausing to reflect, she acted quickly before her niece changed her mind, as she had done several times before.

The first thing she did was to get rid of her fringe that, as she had so often told her niece, made her face look smaller. She had been wearing her hair like this since she was a little girl, but now she was 30 years old. It drove Roberto wild. Many times, after giving Aurora a long, slow kiss on the lips, he would blow her fringe from her forehead to keep close to her for a while longer. Aurora's fringe would fly, and so would Aurora.

Now she was ready for a change.

"I'm leaving tomorrow, Clemente," said Aurora.

"Well, you've taken my words at face value. On my very birthday, off you go . . . And so you should." He regained his composure. "You ought to pass by that agency as soon as possible. That one, and others; you'll see how quickly you'll find a job. A job that'll leave you breathless, so that you'll have to come back here to rest . . ."

If you're not working, rest doesn't do you any good.

Which was why she had to leave. At least that's what Aurora believed. She looked truly beautiful in the eyes of Clemente and all the guests who came to celebrate his birthday and the feast day of the obscure saint who had given his name to their village. San Martín had taken over all the leading roles, and nobody asked about San Clemente any more. Someday soon, the fourth committee would propose looking into his life, after they had finished listening to Bach and debating spiritual questions.

Serving the cake, her short hair combed dramatically back, Aurora looked full of life for the first time in years. Those who were already gossiping about Aurora and Clemente saw her rôle here as kind hostess as more convincing proof of their theory.

That was why everyone was rather surprised when, still holding the serving knife in her hand, Aurora took the floor and made a farewell speech. She told them that it was time for her to go, and that she would be leaving by bus the very next day. She added that she had enjoyed a wonderful time with them all, and that she hoped she could return soon, if her job allowed.

She knew she was going to find a job.

She asked them to take good care of her aunt and uncle, and to take advantage of Clemente's presence in the village. She concluded by saying that they were all very lucky to have him there. She congratulated him on his birthday, and began to clap; her applause was quickly taken up by all the villagers who had responded to the invitation. More would arrive, and others would leave as the house filled up. Some brought cakes with them, so there was plenty for everyone. Almost every villager came, except for Fran, the school teacher, who had to go to Ourense on school business, and Joaquín, who was waiting in the bar for the beer distributor.

The two men also heard the news that Aurora was leaving.

CHAPTER XV

San Clemente de Quintás

22 November 2000

Dear Clemente,

I'm sitting at my Aunt Domi's warming table, with the brazier at my feet and rain outside the window . . . and I'm going to write down a few notes to leave for you on your computer, since that's why you lent it to me, after all.

What a day tomorrow will be for your birthday! And your saint's day, too, and the feast day of the village saint . . . I see that the calendar is filled with saints.

One of my Uncle César's books talks about San Clemente, and I'll tell you about him, in this document named *aurora.doc* – how ugly the names of stories sound on computers!

I admit that I don't really understand the great deeds of the saints, but I think you ought to know that your patron saint (and the village's namesake) was a terrifically disobedient fellow who was sent into exile and condemned to hard labour in the mines. There were two thousand Christians suffering in the same mine, all dying of thirst because it was so extremely dry. Clemente made a spring burst forth from the arid rocks, and many of those who witnessed his deed converted to the faith. That's it, in a nutshell. I hope it does him justice. Pardon the summary.

Is there any literature in the lives of the saints?

I've been thinking about Aurea, who was one of my classmates. She was always the very first to bring sweets to the teacher, almost as soon as the school year began, on October 4, St Aurea's day. My classmate couldn't wait to celebrate her birthday in the summer; instead, she celebrated her patron saint's day. She bragged about her good luck compared to mine, because I didn't know (and still don't) whether there has ever been a saint among all the Auroras in history.

The calendar is full of names. Today is Santa Cecilia, the patron saint of musicians, and I think it makes a good eve for your birthday and saint's day. Thirty-eight, didn't you say?

Music is the closest thing there is to thought. Why are people so afraid of thinking? Why don't they ever leave enough time to reflect? There's nothing wrong with tranquillity; nor emptiness, vertigo, or even unhappiness. I think that these things are the first steps that precede the birth of a new thought. This is why I like to read, as you know, that's the path that I've found easiest to follow.

I haven't even left yet, and I already miss our conversations by the river. What will the villagers have to gossip about now?

I have the feeling that a lot of things await me in Madrid. My own birthday is coming up, too, and I think it's time for me to go back to living. I've learned to live without you-know-who. It isn't bad to remember him, though . . . Lord! I can't even write his name.

We are our blood, we are the people we have seen die, we are the books that have bettered us . . . Someone said that – wasn't it Borges? I don't quite recall, but the fact of the matter is that I've never forgotten those words.

You have also made me believe them.

Happy birthday, Clemente. I wish you many doubts. Don't change, and change us a little; I think that's how we all like you.

A big hug.

Aurora

CHAPTER XVI

It is hard to see the moon in Madrid, and even harder in Aurora's neighbourhood; if you're too careless as you stare up at the night sky, a bus might run you over. She made a last attempt at the entrance to her building. She looked up at the sky, tilting her head to the left, and she was almost doubled over backwards by the time she'd found something up there that looked like a thin nail clipping. This was the kind of moon that received her in Madrid. A new moon. Brand new.

Her letter box was bulging with mail. A fortnight away from Madrid is longer than two weeks away from anywhere else. She could barely manage the suitcase and the bag of plastic containers filled with all the food her Aunt Domi had cooked for her. And now 20 letters, at least.

Five floors to climb. She was practised at resolving the difficulties. The post fell to the floor on the landing outside her flat while she nonchalantly unlocked the door. Carrying her bag and all that packaged food made her lose track of the lightweight letters. An unimportant detail; now that the door was open, she could pick up the envelopes.

She found herself face to face with Fany and a companion wrapped in a bathrobe, in the living room of her flat.

The living room of Aurora's flat is really her whole house: you open the door, and everything that isn't the bedroom, bathroom or kitchen is the living room, the first thing you see when you walk in.

The two of them were eating fried eggs and hearty-looking sausages.

The letters waited where they had landed, scattered across the floor, unconcerned by the shocked faces of all three characters in this scene. Aurora looked down out of sheer curiosity, and her eyes fell on five letters from the agency with Guillermo's name handwritten above the return address.

Fany took advantage of Aurora's distraction to tell Tomás to get dressed while she cleared the dishes and cleaned the table. And herself.

"I'm sorry, Aurora, I had no idea you'd be coming back now, on a Friday night," her neighbour said in a pleading voice.

"Please clear up everything, Fany," Aurora said in a serious tone, not lifting her eyes from the envelopes, but without sounding very angry; she was more interested in her post and in her own life than in other people's business. "I don't want to see anything in there. Let me know when you're done."

And she went to the bathroom. And locked the door.

Fany soon let her know.

"See you, Aurora, we're off," she said from the other side of the bathroom door. Aurora came out.

Fany was truly quick, not only in her thinking but in carrying things out. The house was all in order, and they each had their clothes safely packed in their sports bags; a bottle of cheap sparkling wine was even sticking out of the side pouch on Tomás's bag.

Fany had planned to spend the weekend there with her companion, four floors up from her parents' flat, but seeing how things had turned out, the couple had to emigrate with supper half-eaten, and their weekend plans came to an end early on Friday night.

Their desserts were still sitting there.

"Tell her we left a lot of fruit in the kitchen," Tomás said, looking at Fany but with the intention of letting Aurora hear him.

"I suppose you paid for it," the owner of the house replied. She didn't bother looking at him. Since she hadn't been introduced to him, she wouldn't need to bother to say goodbye.

"Who does your friend think she is? Tell her, Fany! She thinks that, just because she's in her own flat, she can say whatever she likes to me!" said the fruit man from the Mediodía supermarket, raising his voice.

"Come on, Tomás, let's go," said Fany.

"Aren't you going to have a go at this bird?"

"Look, you know what I have to tell you?" said Aurora, looking at Tomás. "That I don't care; all I want is for you two to go, with the fruit or without it. And, Fany, leave me my keys. The party's over."

Aurora knew how to assert herself when she wanted to.

"But you called me a thief!" shouted Tomás, hoping to get a rise out of Fany.

"Fany, she called me a thief!" he said, even louder, looking at his companion and lover.

No comment.

They went downstairs, leaving the dessert behind. Ten o'clock at night, not much money in their pockets; they weren't sure where to go. On the first-floor landing they met Fany's father, who was hurriedly entering the flat. He wanted to catch the second half of the Real Madrid match. That was what saved them. He didn't even really see them. Nothing about them called his attention – not their mussed hair, nor their packed bags, nor the bottle of sparkling wine. Nothing. Not even Tomás.

"Oh, hi, dear." He wouldn't have been any more expressive with any of his neighbours. Not with his wife, either.

Just in case, Fany had quickly thought up a story about helping her fifth-floor neighbour with her luggage (her father knew vaguely that they were friends). She had a whole speech prepared: about Aurora, how she was coming home right now, and so they had run into each other, and here they were going up and down, helping out with the luggage.

But he champed down on his cigar and walked into his house, and no further explanations were called for. He wouldn't have noticed even if she had been barefoot. Few things ever bothered him, other than getting home late to watch a match, or feeling hungry and not finding any bread at hand.

He closed the door, and that was that. Fany pressed herself against the wall so that her mother wouldn't see her. In her mother's mind, Fany was actually where she had said she would be, and where her mother, in turn, had told her husband she was: in the Sierra de Madrid, with her classmates from the beauty school.

Fany had been travelling a lot lately, her mother thought as she served her husband his soup, while he watched his football. There was no opportunity for any kind of a chat between them, so that's where things stayed on the home front, with her husband concentrating on a dangerous foul, while she entertained herself by calculating how many noodles would fit in her soup spoon.

"That would be a good question for a TV contest," Fany's mother said to herself. She loved TV contests.

And she started eating her supper, too.

At that moment, Tomás and his girl were risking their lives on La Castellana Avenue, maintaining a precarious balance on his underpowered scooter and carrying the two sports bags, one of them tucked under each of Fany's arms. After a few hamburgers and two beers, they'd finally decided where to go. Tomás's house was far away, but if the scooter could get them to the McDonalds in Moncloa, they could also manage it on the motorways that would take them to the south of the city.

They were accompanied by the kind of luck that people take for granted and rarely appreciate.

They reached Tomás's block at the same moment Fany's mother was cleaning the kitchen and Aurora was finishing off the last turnip tops from the remains of a pork shoulder stew that she had been eating at the warming table in her aunt and uncle's house the day before.

Each of them, stomachs now full, were wrapped up in their Friday night chores. It seemed impossible that a week could be coming to a close; Aurora still felt in the thick of things, and her face glowed with a light that looked like that at daybreak in Ourense when she used to go to the doctor with her mother. She wasn't even angry at Fany; her neighbour had driven her to distraction many times before. Thanks to her, Aurora had come face to face with the uncomfortable reality of the agency. Perhaps her friend's intrusion into the sanctity of her home was a signal that she should stop trying to hold on to the relics of her past.

She realised that the past would never return, even if it had never entirely gone away.

Fany sank down on to Tomás's unmade bed; Fany's mother sank down into her husband's arms when his match was over. Clemente sank down into a chair at his kitchen table and opened up his laptop, where he found a document called *aurora.doc*.

Aurora sank down on to the sofa, with the five envelopes from Guillermo in her hands. She looked at the postmarks and put the five letters in order. She began with the oldest one: it asked Aurora Ortiz Menéndez to contact the *Talento* Agency upon her return from her trip. The next two repeated the same request. Only the fourth and fifth addressed Aurora in a more personal way. Several pages, written by hand and signed by Guillermo, aroused her curiosity.

If the new moon could have changed its position in the sky, Aurora would have been surprised to see that this heavenly body, which had looked like a thin nail clipping earlier that night, had turned into an electric smile.

CHAPTER XVII

16 November 2000

To: Aurora Ortiz Menéndez
From: Guillermo Fernández Casa

My dear Aurora,

I got your letter yesterday, and I feel that I can no longer write to you in a formal, distant way. Though I haven't had a chance to interview you (or perhaps because I haven't done so), I want to ask you to forgive me. And I don't know how to ask for forgiveness in a business letter.

I am at home, and I'm addressing you by hand. My writing might flag at times, as I find it hard to keep my head straight at this time of night. It is two in the morning. I stayed late at work, and sleep overcame me after supper. You might not believe it, but I put my head down on the kitchen table and slept for two hours, as if I were taking a nap at my school desk. I don't know if they made you take naps like that when you were a child; for us, it was something we did every day: put our heads down on our desks, take our naps. With your own arms as your pillow.

I didn't want to leave your letter for tomorrow, because I'm expecting the work day to be even worse. By eleven in the morning, I have to find the ten warehouse workers I wasn't able to round up today; the Colomar chain asked me to have them on the job by two in the afternoon, so they can start unloading the merchandise that they're expecting from France tomorrow.

Forgive me for telling you all this, it comes out, from sheer frustration, each time I open my mouth. You can never tell what the next minute will bring in my line of work. That is what attracted me to this job from the beginning. Psychologist in charge of selecting personnel for a recruitment agency: no monotony, new challenges all the time, dealing with people . . . I even gladly accepted the extreme situations that came up.

I never imagined, however, when I was studying psychology, that I would end up here. To locate our applicants, I talk with mothers, with grandmothers . . . I am constantly reviewing the people we have on our files, we have them listed for the temporary jobs we can offer them as drivers, delivery men, checkout operators, telesales people, waiters and waitresses . . . But our job applicants never wait for our phone calls. Worse, they are never home, and they hardly ever turn on their cell phones, yet when a company calls on us, they only give us a few hours to find them, to select the right applicants, write up their contracts, get all the legal matters squared away, and make sure they are clean and ready at the time and place at which they are supposed to start working. Set to work for hours, with enthusiasm and efficiency.

In the end, we always work with the same people; we rarely add new workers because, in spite of all the problems, we always manage to accomplish what is asked of us with the personnel that we have on our books. Of course, when someone new walks into the agency, we make a file for them, after one of my colleagues has given them an interview. After that step, we file the person under the appropriate profile in our data bank.

I had my colleague, María José, let Fany know that I

was interested in contacting you; I suppose she must have told you, since I was the one you wrote to.

And you did it to put a full stop to a hiring process that we had never even started.

Your letters have provoked people's curiosity. That is a fact, yet nobody takes you to be something that you are not. At least I do not. More than that: let me tell you that it has been my own sheer selfishness that has kept my colleague from calling you. I kept postponing it for the next day. I wanted to be in charge of your case myself.

For me, your letters were like an oasis of heavenly peace. I'd read them over and over again here at home. I was dying to meet you, though I wasn't sure how I could manage it, because your sense of self has given me the energy I need to get through my working days, which are made up of hours that disappear and cease to exist.

Time doesn't belong to you, it belongs to others. At least that's how it is in my line of work.

I suggested to my colleague that she call Fany to substitute in a job at a beauty salon. I told her to ask about you at the end of the interview, and everything she said filled out the information that I already had gleaned from your letters.

Now I am the one writing to you. I am doing this from my home; I am even sending you my personal address, though you can also contact me through the agency. Call there when you get back in town, and let's set a date so that we can begin the process of finding you what you want.

I hope you understand my explanations.

Guillermo Fernández Casa

*

Aurora didn't give herself so much as two minutes to recover from the contents of the letter she had just read, before she went on to the fifth and final letter, which had arrived just one day earlier. It was also from Guillermo, though this time it was written on his office paper, and so looked much more distant.

22 November

Dear Aurora Ortiz:

My previous letter appears not to have been entirely convincing; nor were my earlier communications.

Perhaps this is the appropriate time to tell you that we have just received a request from a property management firm who are seeking a professional caretaker for a building under their administration.

Please understand that we do not have your profile registered with us, because you have not yet come into our offices for a personal interview, and therefore those on our files will logically be given priority over you.

Please contact the Talento Agency at your earliest convenience; it is of the utmost urgency that my colleague María José or I conduct your hiring interview.

At the foot of the page you will find the address and telephone number of our firm, the Talento Agency.

I hope you have received my earlier communications.

Yours faithfully,

Guillermo Fernández Casa
Psychologist

*

Aurora looked at the time: half-past ten on Friday night. She went outside; the moon was hiding behind the buildings. She ran to the agency. There was scarcely any light inside, just a faint glimmer from deep within the building, but all the doors were locked.

She rang the number from the phone booth in front. Rang it again. No answer. But the light still burned. She stood there for an hour, as cold as she had felt the night she waited for Fany outside the Mediodía supermarket. Her hands grew stiff; her bones. Her whole body.

Fifteen minutes after the last time she had looked at her watch, the slatted metal gate over the entrance was raised, creating a screech that called for a drop of oil, or at least a bit of attention.

It was the cleaning ladies. Contractors who had finished their job. Aurora approached them.

"Do you know whether Guillermo, the psychologist, is inside?" she asked.

"There's nobody left in there," said the oldest of the four.

Good thing the moon was in hiding. If it hadn't been, she would have seen how it looked: an inverted smile, beaten, worn out. Nor was there a single star in the sky, not one of those stars that augurs that tomorrow will be a fine day, that the sun will be shining; a cloudless day.

Not a single star. Aurora remembered as she looked up at the sky. She had liked doing this since she was a child: searching for the aurora borealis, even though she wasn't quite sure just what it was.

At night in Madrid, where there is nothing but traffic in the streets and not a single light in the starless sky, you feel thankful when a bit of traffic appears up there, too.

And so it happened. A blinking light flashed slowly across the dark sea of the sky. It was a plane. Aurora followed it with her eyes. It was the best thing she managed to see on that endless Friday night in November.

CHAPTER XVIII

"Good morning," Aurora said to the receptionist at the *Talento* Agency, scarcely giving her a chance to set down her bag behind her chair – the first thing she did every morning when she arrived at work.

"Good morning," she replied, as if to say, "Here we go again . . ." though Aurora had to admit she had a pleasant enough face.

"I was hoping to see Guillermo Fernández Casa. It's about a job interview," said Aurora, at three minutes past nine in the morning.

"Did you have an appointment? I don't see anything written down here in Guillermo's diary. If you want to be interviewed, you have to make an appointment . . ."

"Look, this is a fairly urgent matter, because it's about a job that they want filled right away," Aurora was trying to convince the receptionist when, at that very moment, a woman of about 30 appeared at the door.

"Good morning, María José," said the receptionist.

Aurora didn't give the intermediary another second.

"Hello, María José, I'm Aurora, the one who's been writing to you about a finding a job as a caretaker. Guillermo told me that there's a possible position, and he told me to come in for an interview with you or with him." Aurora spoke with all the enthusiasm she could muster.

"But wasn't he going to do the interview?" the psychologist listlessly asked Pilar, the receptionist, who was also feeling listless on that Monday morning.

"I dunno . . . I was telling this lady that she'd have to make an appointment before coming in for an interview. But, in any case, Guillermo's first appointment is at eleven o'clock this morning. He was going to go over to the trade fair before coming in today, so he could confirm that all the hostesses reported to work and finish up with the client. I don't think it should take him more than an hour."

"Well, then," said María José, looking at Aurora with a touch of disdain. For a psychologist, she was a bit too easily put out when something upset her schedule.

"Fine," she said, now addressing only the receptionist. "Tell her to fill out all the forms, and then she'll have to wait for me. I'll get started on the interview, and when Guillermo comes in, he can take over. As soon as he comes in," she said with emphasis, and sounding rather upset, "tell him that he's in charge of this case, just as we agreed. I don't understand a bit of it, to tell you the truth. I'm going to my office now. Let me know when the forms are all filled out."

Aurora found herself holding a blue ballpoint pen and a pile of papers covered with blanks for her to fill in. If only it had been one of those crossword puzzle books she sometimes bought at the kiosk on Bravo Murillo – a book that gives you the answers on the last page, forcing you to use all your willpower to resist the temptation to peek at the place where everything is given away. All the questions, perfectly answered.

Here, feeling lost between these white walls and time-worn cobalt-blue desks, she sat down where the receptionist told her to, at a table with five chairs, facing a wall. For an instant she thought she was in the doctor's office in Ourense; that room was just as antiseptic as this one here, scrubbed to a bleached-out bluish white.

Sometimes, things can be so clean they hurt. Immaculate, yet hostile.

"We have to operate, Pura; we must try to stop the tumour from spreading," the doctor had told her mother. He and the nurse were dressed in white from head to toe.

Aurora was wearing green, the honeycomb dress that her mother always dressed her in when they went to the city. Her mother was wearing a suit in the same colour.

"Hope is evergreen, dear," Pura had said to her on the bus, with a cheerfulness that she couldn't have faked.

But it was false that the green could provide more chances for life. It was only by coincidence that Aurora was also wearing green today: green trousers, and a checked shirt with a green background.

"Fill in all these forms as completely as you can, and ask me if you have any questions. Let me know when you're done." With this, the receptionist wrapped up the conversation and left Aurora alone, so that she could finally get back into the full swing of her morning routine.

Pilar set her bag down behind her desk at the entrance to the agency. She took out her tissues, sugarless sweets and a packet of black liquorice. And she took a deep breath as she looked out the window – more a display window or a showcase than a simple office window. The working week was beginning. A new day. The neighbourhood women were going out to do the shopping, and the blind lottery ticket salesman, who turned his back on her every morning as she passed him on the footpath, had come out earlier than usual; she saw that he had been blessed by lady luck, because three women (who didn't look like they lived in the neighbourhood) had each bought two tickets from him before stopping for coffee and *porras* at the café next door.

"Come on, Aurora, let's hope for the best," Aurora was telling herself meanwhile, as she began to fill in all those blanks.

It seemed easy, at least the section on personal information did: first name, last name, place, province, date of birth . . . She had to write her mother's name. And her father's. She even knew it, though it made her boil with such anger it was a wonder the ink didn't evaporate from the pen – having to write down the name of a man she wouldn't have recognised even if he were sitting here in front of her. Writing down her current address, city, province, and contact phone numbers helped calm her down again.

Foreign workers would have to keep filling out this section of the form: passport number, work permit number, date issued, expiration date. Aurora felt relieved – she could go on to the next section. About her education.

Here she began to mark fewer boxes. She didn't mind ticking the "no" box when it came to the questions about having a driver's licence or a car. She didn't have either.

Nevertheless, she found it hard to leave most of the choices blank when it came to indicating the level that she had reached in her official studies (last year completed, date of completion of last course, titles obtained, speciality) and everything pertaining to advanced studies or college or university degrees or professional diplomas, or O levels, or A levels, or any kind of technical or master's degree . . . Indeed a great many possibilities were listed. After she had read all the way to the bottom and back up again to the top of the page, she determined that the only one that applied to her at all was the very last, and to some extent the next-to-last.

She circled General Basic Education. There was no space for her to indicate that her grades had been excellent, that she had been a promising student, that she was a hard-working young girl with limitless curiosity, that she had loved looking at tadpoles in puddles and that, had she been able, she might have studied the sciences, perhaps biology, though in reality she changed her mind every day.

She also ticked off the box for secondary education; she had studied at the school in Lonxo for three years, something which in itself implied a great effort on her family's part. She marked the year in which she had completed the final course. There was no space here, either, for indicating her good grades, nor for pointing out that what she really had wanted to do during those years was to study Latin more deeply. She loved nothing more than to dissect *The Conspiracy of Cataline* and put its inner workings up for display, phrase by phrase, on the blackboard. She especially liked slicing up thoughts with chalk.

She always loved thoughts and thinking, with or without chalk.

When her girlfriends started wandering off into the thick forest in that part of Ourense province with boys from their class, she would stay behind in the school library. It was there that she first started reading.

And reading was as far as she got. Everyone who could, left for the city to take the university preparatory classes and continue towards a university degree. Only three of her classmates ended up in the city of Ourense, and later on at university in Santiago: Mario, Berta and Julia. They each studied law, and they are still working in Santiago, in the legal department of a consumers' rights office.

All the rest, including Aurora, stayed behind in the village – not even in Lonxo, just San Clemente. Each one of them helped their parents in the family business, whether a farm or another occupation. Aurora watched over her mother when her Aunt Domi was in the hairdresser's, and she took care of the hairdresser's when Aunt Domi was with her mother.

She spent more and more time in her aunt's shop. Her mother's illness prolonged her stay among the hair dyes and scissors. It was there that Roberto appeared one day; her future husband was very wary of her untrained haircutting hands.

He got to know those hands well, by dancing with her in the village square of San Clemente and from kidding her in the Lonxo hairdresser's. And he didn't stop joking with her until he had placed a wedding band on the fourth finger of her hand, counting from the thumb. The fourth finger of her right hand.

By then, her mother had died, and she left the hairdresser's for ever. She had never liked it, and all it brought her was the anguished memory of the telephone, which rang but seldom, yet often enough to make Aurora toss down her combs and, with her heart racing, try to calm herself before picking up the receiver. She never knew whether it would be someone calling from the hospital to tell her that her mother was dying, or just a woman calling from the village to ask when she could come in to dye her greying hair.

The hairdresser's was her one and only work experience, but she never spoke of it. The sheets of the *Talento* Agency's form hadn't asked her about it yet, either. There were still plenty of blanks to fill in about her education. Later on, she told herself.

No, she hadn't taken any other courses worth mentioning; no course of study to expand or improve upon what she had already noted in the section above. The spaces for writing the name of the course, its duration and date, the institution attended, and the titles or certificates achieved, also remained blank. A whole new expanse of white space and unmarked boxes told the truth about the holes in her education.

She quickly turned to the next sheet, and found the questions about languages.

Aurora hadn't expected these; not that it was unusual for them to ask, but the possibility had never occurred to her. Seeing this new section gave her a sense of vertigo, like the first time she dived into the village pond from the highest rock, straight into the water. She would never finish falling, the suspense was endless.

That was how she imagined eternity: falling endlessly, except that one would have control over gravity.

Clemente couldn't help laughing when Aurora explained her theory about the beyond to him.

Three blanks to fill in about languages. Rate on a scale from 1 to 5 your facility at speaking, listening and reading. Also indicate where you studied this language or that, and the length of study. She skipped over the rest of the blanks and scored herself on Galician, rating herself a bit on the high side, to tell the truth.

Typing and shorthand. Nothing. She did tick *yes* on the third section, about computer use. With her tick marks, she explained that she was a regular computer user (both desktop and laptop, she dared add). Then she figured she could skip a few questions that she didn't understand, which asked about her level of competence in two items, labelled in English: *hardware* and *software*.

As for her current job situation, she ticked off the box that said she was not working at the moment, as well as the one that said she was not on the dole. They didn't ask about her widow's pension, even though they had known since page 1 that she was a widow.

The last sheet was all about her work experience. She was supposed to explain in full detail every firm for which she had ever worked; the functions she had performed; the rates of compensation she had received; when she had changed jobs, and why. She was also supposed to include contact telephone numbers. And a whole sheet of paper just for this. She realised how many jobs some applicants must have held. Not her.

She only mentioned the hairdresser's, in general terms. Two years in total; salary varying according to the amount of time she worked.

In the section about her experience with other agencies she also left a considerable blank space. This was her first time. Then again, in the slight space set aside to ask about the hours she could work, she didn't skimp on the tick-marks. She made it clear that her time was completely free; not a single box remained unmarked where she was to indicate her preferred work times. Every hour was exactly the same, because she could think just as well in the morning as in the afternoon or at night. And every day of the week, yes. Nor would she have any problem working, not only from Monday to Friday every month of the year, but also during every public holiday. Any holiday at all.

This seemed to inspire her. So much so that she felt confident as she rejected almost every option in the next and final section. It asked her about various specialisations; she was to specify which of them might fit with her tastes and abilities. She rejected them all. Administrative assistant, bookkeeper, telephone receptionist, secretary, database manager, draughtsman, hostess, warehouse clerk, word processor, fork-lift operator, clerk 1, clerk 2, clerk 3, telesales person, sales promoter, checkout operator, stocker, maid, cleaning woman, driver . . . Not a tick.

Fortunately, there was an option for "Other positions". What a display of consideration this Section 5 was for those who felt more lost or more insecure, perhaps, or else supremely sure of themselves. Aurora wrote, in capital letters, the option that none of the listed categories had mentioned: caretaker of a building.

In the final leg of this chore, she found a short space set aside for any pertinent observations that the job applicant might wish to make, just before signing to certify that every piece of information contained in this form was true and current, and also to authorise the *Talento* Agency to computerise all of the above.

"So much writing, to get so little information," Aurora thought. Just four tick-marks in all the spaces for describing her education and professional experience. The section on the times she would be available to work raised her tick count, but she really ought to write something in the observation section. She couldn't imagine what. That, too, remained blank.

So she signed. She hadn't noticed, but she had spent a long time looking at the wall and at the blank paper. Almost an hour; María José had stood up from her desk at one point to look at Aurora through the metal blinds that gave her office a touch of privacy. She saw her, still sitting there, back turned, writing little.

The psychologist looked at her watch. She seemed happy; with a little luck, Guillermo would arrive soon, and she would be free of a person who had no place in her plans, nor her schedule, nor her thoughts, not even in the slightest, most distant way. She, along with the office supervisor – they were good friends and liked sharing a joke – had been the most dedicated mockers of the words Aurora had used in her letters. "What next? Oh, dear me! What next?" they would ask between guffaws, when María José read out loud the latest news from the woman who now sat two paces away from her desk.

There, dressed in green trousers and a checked blouse, Aurora stood up and went to let the receptionist know that she was all done. Pilar had forgotten all about her. Twelve phone calls, four faxes, and the roar of the roadworks have a way of distancing one a bit from the tranquillity of the inner sanctum of the offices.

CHAPTER XIX

"Come in," said María José. "Take a seat."

"Thank you," Aurora replied, choosing between the two office chairs in front of her.

"Have you brought a recent photograph?" asked María José, although these minor questions are always left for the end of the interview.

She took her time beginning the detailed questioning of the person sitting in front of her. She looked at her watch and then took it off and put it where she could see it, on her desk. She usually did this before she began the interview but today María José was doing it for a hidden reason – in the hope of running down the clock. Guillermo could arrive any moment and relieve her of this person, for whom he had shown from the beginning a particular and, to María José, incomprehensible sympathy.

"Let's see if he doesn't dawdle," María José thought impatiently, when she saw that the psychologist who worked in the office next door, and with whom she had nothing in common, was still not back.

She had no choice but to begin, as if there were no other job applicants in the world, nor (of course) any other psychologist who could help Aurora.

"OK, Aurora – we can go by first names here – tell me as much as you'd like, as if I were a good friend of yours and you were just talking. And, please, let's go by first names, informally, just as if I were your friend, remember. First, where were you born, and what kind of work would you like to have?"

She looked again at her watch.

Aurora could have sworn that just before this speech, María José had been speaking to her in a very formal and distant way, but she wasn't allowed the time to stop and recall the previous scene. What should she say? She answered with another question – something said to be very common among Galicians.

"Did you not read my letters?"

A question like this, posed at the very outset of the interview by someone who had left four pages of the questionnaire practically blank, struck María José as being, without any doubt, in untenably bad form.

"Just pretend that I don't remember any of it," her interrogator hit back.

"I am a good applicant for a job as a building caretaker."

"I know." María José took in a deep breath and smiled when she let it out, so that it would not be too obvious how irritated she was.

She waited for an answer. None came.

Aurora realised that she was doing very badly, but she didn't know how to change things. It wasn't hard to guess that, if someone at the agency had thought she was crazy (as Fany had insinuated), this someone was María José. Indeed, this woman facing her would have thrown away her letters if Guillermo hadn't stopped her.

She began to get up from her chair, then sat down again. Aurora wanted to give herself a second chance.

"I see you have finished your secondary school studies." The *Talento* psychologist tried to give her a hand.

"Yes, I studied humanities at the school in Lonxo, in Ourense province, near my home village."

"Ah, so you're Galician," María José said, though both of them knew full well that was what she was. "I often spend the summer up there in Galicia, at the beaches around Playa America."

"Yes, that whole area's quite nice. My own village is rather more inland. The beaches I'm familiar with are the ones further north, in Lugo and up there; they are also very nice. I used to go there with my mother sometimes, though we were never able to stay long."

"Oh, that's what they call the *Costa de la Muerte*, the Coast of Death, isn't it?" María José peeked amiably at her watch.

"Yes. That is, as far as I'm concerned, yes, it is, though the Coast of Death actually starts a bit to the west." Aurora began to relax a little. It seemed as if her mother's ghostly hand was trying to help her . . . However, her quickness in answering began to bother her questioner again.

"So, when you lived inland there in Ourense, what did you used to do? What did you like to do?"

"Those are two separate questions, if you don't mind my saying so."

"We're just friends here, please," María José insisted again.

"What I used to do was what I liked doing, up until I finished secondary school. After that, I lazed around for a while up there in my village, and then I started doing what I didn't like to do, which was working at the hairdresser's. I was an assistant hairdresser for two years; I did everything from giving highlights with silver paper, to putting hair in curlers, to doing a complete perm. I wasn't as good with the scissors, but I could more or less handle them, especially men's haircuts."

"We could have interviewed you for the job that we called your friend in for. And on top of it, she said no at the last minute, and I don't know whether we ever filled that position. Do you know how to give massages, too?"

"No, I don't. I don't want a job in a beauty salon. I don't enjoy it, and I don't think I would be good at it."

"You'd do your best, I imagine . . . Forgive me for asking a rather personal question. You're a widow, according to this box you've marked here, correct?"

"Yes, I am. Three years now."

"May I ask you how you make a living? I mean, apart from the pension I imagine you're receiving."

"I live on the pension that Renfe gives me, but it all goes towards paying the mortgage for the flat we bought when we got married. Well, I still have a bit left over for buying food and whatnot. I get a small allowance for taking care of the children of Ecuadorian women, the ones who live around this district. It's a parish initiative. I help them, and they help me."

"Those Ecuadorians! There are a lot of them around here, aren't there?" María José tried to soften her tone. "Some of them come here to see us, but of course, if they have no work permit we can't do much to help them. True, the ones who have all their papers in order have never given us any trouble. They're good workers, whether as couriers or unloading boxes in a warehouse somewhere; or we'll send them to Murcia for the fruit harvest. Let me tell you, there's all the difference in the world between one of these people and our own 'boys with toys', who just want to pick up a little extra cash for the summer. Beginning with that little detail of punctuality. Punchality is the most important thing when you're on a job, but our young men can't seem to be bothered with setting their alarm clocks. Imagine how eager they are to work! That's what happens when you don't really need a job . . ."

"Aurora, you must need to work, right?" the psychologist added, looking into her eyes and asking her to answer the question in all confidence.

"Since my husband died three years ago, I've spent most of my time putting my life in order. I've spent the rest of it writing to you to ask for help in finding a job – first by hand, then by computer, when I started getting some help and was able to borrow one. Neither of these two things have been expensive; I don't need much money to live, and I'm used to what I already have. But, I do need to work."

"Reading your letters, you give the impression of being – how could I put it? – a girl with a whim; it seems you only want one job, as a caretaker, and to top it all off, you have no previous experience in the field."

"I know I'd do it well."

"But wouldn't you also do well at anything else, for the same salary, such as, I don't know, a telephone receptionist, a telesales person, a waitress, or a cleaning lady? There are lots of jobs you could do, but you haven't even marked them."

"I wouldn't be qualified for them," Aurora replied.

"And who told you that? You, yourself?" the psychologist asked in astonishment. "Aurora, you don't seem to need a job. I don't know whether we've covered that caretaker's position that we were asked to fill last week – Guillermo will look into it when he gets back – but, believe me, I find it hard to imagine that you would want to limit your possibilities so much. This way, it could take you another three years."

"Right . . .," Aurora said with resignation.

"Right," the psychologist repeated. She was beginning to think that the person in front of her needed another kind of help, not the kind that you could find here at this firm, even though she was a psychologist. "I don't know whether you're aware that the young people today, even those who are highly educated, with university degrees," she said, picking up the blank pages of her applicant's form, "have a very difficult time when it comes to finding their first job; they pay their dues by working on temporary or part-time contracts. If you're over 50, you're as good as condemned to permanent unemployment; between the ages of 26 and 40, your chances grow utterly dim. And that's without even going into the details of the female workforce, the most afflicted sector in the world of unemployment."

"How old did you say you were, Aurora?" she asked, looking back at the first page of the form.

"I'm 30," Aurora replied.

"Thirty. Look, now, Aurora," she continued to harangue. "Jobs are quite scarce. The unemployment rate is hovering around 15 per cent among Spanish men and women who are old enough to work for their daily bread . . . People are being forced into retirement before their children have even left home, and 60-year-olds don't like feeling useless in society, but the fact of the matter is that, in the end, the parents and the children end up sitting together in the living room – the parents, because they've been kicked back into their house, and their children, because they've never been able to leave it. The other day, just to give you an example of what I'm talking about, Aurora, a fellow went so far as to offer a kidney for sale on the radio – a kidney in exchange for a job.

"A *job*, Aurora. Any old job, not the job you've been waiting for all your life, which is what you seem to have in mind. And I'm talking about a fellow who was – what? – 50 or 55 years old. With who knows how many years of experience behind him. Do you know what I'm saying?"

"Yes." It was the first time Aurora had said yes.

She was defeated.

That was how Guillermo found her when he abruptly threw open the door of his colleague's office, though he actually didn't know what she usually looked like; he had never seen Aurora, just read her letters. Over and over again, many times. And he had written several letters of his own to her. Once even to beg her forgiveness, something that everyone at the agency would have regarded as excessive, had he sought their opinion.

You should never let yourself get involved in an applicant's life. That was the basic rule of his business. Which was why he did it without asking for advice.

It infuriated him that he hadn't even imagined that Aurora might be at the office. In his haste, he hadn't thought of his own interests, but had he known that she'd been at the agency for two hours already, Guillermo would have rushed his conversation with his client – the one at the trade fair – even more, even if it were only to gain a few scant minutes. Preparing 15 hostesses to begin the work day, and leaving everything in order for them and for his client: there was an absolute minimum amount of time that you had to spend on a job like that. He had fulfilled the task with scrupulous exactitude, once more.

His scooter brought him back to his office faster than he could have managed by public transport. Guillermo had convinced his firm to pay for his petrol, thereby saving time, during the five years he had been working there.

As he entered, Pilar said to him, "Hey there, handsome" – which is what she always called him, though by now she had given up on him as a failed conquest. He didn't pay her any attention, not even on Fridays, when things were a bit more relaxed. "Hey, handsome," she said again, though today she said it with something else in mind, "you really dropped María José in it."

"What's up?" he asked, as he put his helmet away in the wardrobe by the entrance.

"The girl who wants to be a caretaker, the bore who wrote all the letters – she's been with María José for a whole hour. She said she'd leave the girl to you as soon as you came in."

Guillermo ran straight down the corridor. He opened the door and saw two women of about the same age thinking about something just said. There was a kind of tension in María José's expression. She looked at Guillermo and couldn't help brightening in spite of it all. She decided to help him out, one more time.

"Guillermo, why don't you take over from here. She's barely started talking to me," she said in a pretentiously amiable tone. "I'll take your eleven o'clock interview; mine got cancelled."

"Thanks," Guillermo said with all his heart. Perhaps his colleague had more virtues than he had been able to discover in her over these five years.

"We can go to my office, Aurora." He made a gesture of helping her lightly from her chair.

Music from the radio that Pilar had just turned on was wafting down the corridor. Time to take a break for some of the bitter coffee from the machine. It was truly bitter, especially that first sip; no amount of sugar packets was capable of countering such intensity.

> *I wish I could drink but not forget,*
> *I wish I could be happy and start it all again.*
>
> *I wish I were the sea, but all I have is foam.*
> *I wish I could go on, but all I have is foam.*
> *I can't make it without you, won't you give me a hand.*
> *All I have is doubt.*
>
> *I wish I were the sea, but all I have is foam.*

The music faded into the depths of the corridor when Guillermo shut the door of his office. This time Aurora didn't spend any time considering which of the chairs to sit in; either of them was fine.

"How's things?" Guillermo asked her with a smile, flushed from a morning that had been no less busy than any other . . .

"Excuse me," he suddenly added, and he stood back up. "I'm going to go tell Pilar to watch my scooter, because I left it on the pavement next to the entrance." He rushed out the door.

Again she heard the radio. This time it was an Enrique Bunbury song. He was asking someone, very gently, how, "if we have the same fate, the same desires as ever, if we're going the same way . . . even if we're tumbling through this world . . ." how can it still be that . . .

> *How can you ask if we have anything in common?*

And it asked again,

> *how can you ask if we have anything in common?*

Aurora strained to hear the lyrics. She thought she could make it out: "If we have the same sense of humour and the same discontents, the same sorrows and the same years misspent, the same sense of hope . . ." Then, why . . . Why even ask . . .

> *How can you ask if we have anything in common?*

The office door closed again. Guillermo was back inside; he was quick. Very quick; energetic. Wide awake, too. Wide awake, but tired. His skin was the colour of the chestnut trees in the orchard in San Clemente; his eyes were a changing shade of brown. There were shadows on every part of his face where there were hollows, especially under his eyes. He was down, but not out. He didn't even know it himself, so busy was he, so hyper, today as much as the day before. Aurora intuited it, even though he had only been sitting quietly behind the desk for five minutes. Just five minutes, looking at her full in the face, silently, relaxed now he knew that his scooter was safe and that he was in good company.

"How's things, Aurora?" He didn't look away. "Here, at last . . ."

She didn't reply.

It had been some time since she last felt this protected. It was almost like when she held her hands out to the bonfire on San Martín's night; the same warmth she felt when she used to sit close to her mother, watching television, snuggled tight under a single blanket on the sofa.

But sometimes a sudden warmth after a chill can be upsetting; Aurora remembered the time she'd frozen her thumb one winter. It had turned purple before she held it up to the kitchen fire to warm it. The pins and needles were unbearable; so uncomfortable it almost made her nauseous.

How's things . . . She heard it in the distance, though she was also looking him in the face. No, things weren't OK. After spending an hour exposed to the iciness and hopelessness of his colleague in the office next door, Guillermo's sad eyes, gazing at her, made her feel something she never would have wished.

It wasn't that she was crying. To be more precise, what was happening was that she couldn't stop a torrent of tears that were on their way. She looked at the floor in order to concentrate, and forced her mind to focus in a way she hadn't for years; all her strength was centred on halting her tears, and failing that, on squeezing her eyelids shut. She wished she could turn them into great iron floodgates so that, by closing them, she might stop up the water that was flowing out. No leaks. She didn't manage it; she was aware of this even before she saw that one drop had already hit the greyish laminated floor.

She didn't dare raise her head. But she didn't need to.

Guillermo sat down in the office chair next to hers, and handed her a paper tissue. It wasn't the first time someone had ever cried in his office . . . but it was the first time he had wanted to embrace a stranger whom he found tremendously familiar.

CHAPTER XX

"Sorry. What an embarrassing situation. In the end, it's going to turn out that I really am a bit crazy," said Aurora. She dried her tears and quickly composed herself, as if she had experienced nothing more serious than a bout of sneezing.

"Do you know anyone who isn't?"

"All right, you psychologists are famous for thinking that way . . . What can I say."

"I'm going to get us a couple of Cokes from the machine, and then we'll start the interview, OK?" he said, already on his way out the door.

Starting all over, explaining her whole life; but Aurora felt fine. Whatever she had to talk about, she'd talk about. She was in good company; in fact, she had a very pleasant sensation of being coddled and sheltered. What she would find unbearable would be if Guillermo were to disappear suddenly again – if he were called to go on another mission; if any unforeseen incident were to make him dash off on his scooter.

Good thing he came back.

Two cold cans of Coke, one in each hand; he closed the door behind him with his foot, almost like a footballer kicking in a goal, the kind Fany's father cheered in front of his TV. Guillermo looked at his watch: eleven-thirty in the morning; and, as he sat down again at his desk, he mentioned that perhaps it was too early for a Coke. A hot cup of coffee would hit the spot . . .

But, he told Aurora, the coffee that the office machine made was awful. It didn't occur to him to suggest stepping out to the corner cafeteria for a cup: that would have been completely out of professional bounds.

Nor did Aurora tell him that everything was perfectly fine.

"Well, for now I won't be asking you anything; just talk to me," Guillermo said with a strange mix of formality and eagerness.

"Hello, I'm Aurora," she began, half-joking. "I was born 30 years ago in the province of Ourense. As I have written on the sheets of paper that are lying over there, my entire education amounts to the years I spent in my village school and at the secondary school in Lonxo, in the next village. When I finished my studies at secondary school, some of my teachers, especially the Latin teacher, told me that I would do very well at law; the art teacher talked to me about studying fine arts; the physics and chemistry teacher (even though I had opted to study humanities) reminded me about the sense of observation and sensibility that, well, she used to say," Aurora blushed, "that I had . . . had developed since I was a young girl. When I saw her in the corridor, she would remind me of my natural gift for the sciences; I could study something like pharmacology, she'd tell me."

"And what did you think about that?"

"Well, I . . . I loved hearing it. Sometimes I even went out of my way so that she'd run into me and tell me so all over again."

"So was pharmacology what you liked the most?"

"What I liked was thinking I was competent. It's a bit hard to explain; I liked it when people saw me as competent. I stretched things out as long as I could before my teachers found out I was another girl who was going to stay in the village. I didn't want them to know that, for me, classes were going to end right there. Living with that mistaken understanding made me a little less miserable; it would have hurt me tremendously if they had found out that I wasn't going to keep on studying, because if they had known it, I would have known it, too."

"Did it hurt you to think they might find out, or was it painful because you wouldn't be able to keep studying?"

"Well, I . . . Nothing in the world would have made me happier. But everything is far away from my village, and distance is expensive – very expensive; when you leave home, you have to sleep somewhere, find a place to stay . . . In my house, the whole notion was out of the question. At that time, there was just my mother, who was already very ill, and Domi, who took care of her. We would take turns. Her husband, César, worked in the National Savings Bank branch in Lonxo, but the two of them were already making a huge effort to send their son, my cousin Anselmo, to study at the Faculty of Arts at Santiago de Compostela. Even so, they helped pay for my books and materials at secondary school."

"And what would you have studied? You still haven't told me."

"I never answered that question myself. I don't know. I thought about unattainable degrees, courses of study that they didn't have at Ourense or even at Santiago. It was a way to suffer less," Aurora said, fixing her eyes on him. "Oceanography, aviation . . . Every day I'd dream up something else."

"How wonderful!" Guillermo said, calmly; registering the extent to which Aurora was surprising him. "What did your teachers say? How did they react?" He couldn't help being swept along by the conversation, though the questions he was asking were completely unnecessary.

"My Latin teacher mentioned that village school teachers are used to seeing few rewards from their labour. At least, that's what he told me when he found out that I was staying there, too. He told me that he was more frustrated than I was, and that someday I would understand him. I haven't had many teachers, but without a doubt he was the best of them. He accompanied me many times to the library; he was there when the municipality of Lonxo gave me a library card, through a special arrangement with the public library in Ourense.

"Until they sent him off to Pontevedra, he took me to the library to return books and get out new ones once a fortnight, and we'd have long conversations about the books that I'd read. My teacher used to tell me that you find the best books in small libraries with small budgets, because, as they don't have the money to buy the latest bestsellers, they have to make do with the classics. I still remember the time he asked me, 'Aurora, see here.'" Aurora pulled a serious face, arching her eyebrows. "'Have you read *Don Quixote?*'

"'Yes,' I answered.

"'Have you?' he asked again. 'Have you read it, or do you just think you've read it?'" She exaggerated the change in voice. "'Everybody thinks he knows *Don Quixote*; one thing is what you hear about it, or what you happen to read – some random chapter – but another thing is truly to have read *Don Quixote*.' And then he asked me the question again." Aurora finished imitating the serious tone that made her face, even her whole being, seem so ingenuous.

But now she replied in her own voice. "I was mistaken. I too was one of those people who hadn't really read *Don Quixote*.

"And so these library loan periods, two weeks at a time, helped me to accept the fact that my year would never again be divided into school terms. That was a good end for a student's life."

"You never know. Perhaps now you could . . . make up for lost time."

"Time can never be made up, but I also don't think that it is ever completely lost. I've also been very happy, believe me." Aurora smiled slightly. "Now I just look ahead."

"Could you say what the happiest moment of your life was? If you had to pick one, what would you tell me?"

"I'm not sure. Sometimes I'm happy even though I'm sad, and sometimes I'm sad even though I'm laughing out loud and telling jokes with a beer in my hand. Happiness depends on the effort you put into being happy rather than something else."

She looked at Guillermo to see whether he thought the same, but she couldn't read his expression.

"When I came to Madrid as a newly-wed, with my husband Roberto, I was happy. We bought a small flat behind this building, and we had our whole lives ahead of us. Everything was in the future. Now I've lost him, and I've only now learned how to be happy even so. I'm happy because that's what I want to be. Don't you think that's the most important thing?"

"Right now, I'm very happy, too," Guillermo said, unblinking.

"And if not, so what, right? It's not such a tragedy not to be happy. Happiness isn't the only thing around. There are so many things . . ."

"Life's a giant puzzle."

Aurora was surprised by his words. She realised that Guillermo had read all her letters from beginning to end; he had learned first-hand of her limitless love for Roberto, her childhood, her neighbour, her whole life . . . She was embarrassed that she'd sealed the very essence of herself in those envelopes.

He guessed what she was thinking. It wasn't hard to notice the half-blush on her cheeks.

"Do you get lots of letters?" *Like mine*, Aurora meant.

"None at all. People come in here and fill those forms."

"Wow . . ."

"After all, you didn't pick the quickest way."

"I bet the caretaker's job, the job at the building that you mentioned in your letter . . . I bet it's already taken. Well, in any case, you still don't know whether I'm qualified for the position or not."

"You're qualified for anything you put your mind to, Aurora. What I don't understand is why you're so set on sitting in a caretaker's office."

"I'd like to travel. In a caretaker's office, I could visit places through books, get to know new civilisations, study the classics, travel around the globe . . . I think it's an appropriate job. I like working, believe me; but sitting at that desk, I'd have lots of dead time. That time would be mine. I'd leave that house on Bravo Murillo – I don't want to live there any more; I'd sell it and pay off the rest of the mortgage, and I'd start living in the rooms that they usually give to the caretaker. Isn't that how it works?"

"Aurora . . . Most of the people who come here are weighed down by a terrible frustration, because their aspirations don't coincide with the opportunities that life has to offer them. They have their sights set, shall we say, somewhat higher than what they can really achieve. And they resent it. You, on the other hand, have tremendously limited your aspirations. And that's another form of . . ."

"I haven't studied at university; I don't have a degree," Aurora said.

"You should start thinking about everything you do have."

"Your colleague was talking to me about jobs in cleaning, telesales, marketing, about . . . I remember now, she was also telling me that the job situation is terrible, and that one fellow even went on the radio, offering to trade a kidney for a job."

"Think about what you want, and fight to get it. *We'll* fight to get it," he said with not altogether convincing enthusiasm.

"I've never been able to think about myself. I've found it impossible. The most I've been able to do has been to take advantage of every conceivable opportunity that's come my way. The only choice I made on my own was when I said yes to Roberto. That was the one and only time. Then we came to Madrid, and I ended up alone. I ended up alone in this city, and now I don't belong here, and I don't belong there. This city is too big, and there are too many people who are good at too many things . . ."

"Such as you."

"And what if being a caretaker is what really appeals to me?"

"Then more power to you. You should know better than anyone."

"I don't know . . . What I hold clearest in my mind are all the things I've done without really wanting to do them, such as cutting hair, leaving off my studies, never spending a term at a residence hall in Santiago, not taking a trip two years before starting to work, not travelling even if I had to go on foot, not having friends all over the world after visiting dozens of countries . . . I often want to talk to people while I'm waiting in the queue for the bus or on the Metro. Lots of people read on the Metro, you know? But, no – they'd also think I was mad, I've figured that much out. I realise that doing any of those things – expressing yourself freely, discussing issues, drawing comparisons – they're the sort of things that people only do when they're on holiday."

Guillermo laughed. "You're so funny . . ."

"It's true!" Aurora said. "They go off and, when they come back, they talk about how wonderful people are on the other side of the world. But when they've finished telling their stories, they stick their heads back in their shells, like when you touch a turtle on the head – isn't it true, its reflex action is to protect itself immediately? I only went on holiday once in my life, on my honeymoon, and to be perfectly frank, we didn't talk to anybody. Of course, it was the circumstances; we didn't want to be disturbed." Aurora grew more animated the more she talked. "If I were to go on a trip now, though . . . Well, and even without going anywhere . . . But I thought you were all my best friends, from the first letter I wrote! I was imagining your faces."

"I got to know you right away. Then I wanted to know you better," Guillermo said, taking advantage of the fact that she was talking and trying not to attach any importance to his words. "The working world is tough."

"I can't travel, and I don't have a lot of people around to talk to, except for the Ecuadorian women I help. So I read. Yes, that must be why I like to read . . ." Aurora was learning something about herself with this new line of thought. "But you're right, the working world has got to be tough, you're right." Guillermo thought that she hadn't heard him.

"What does your office normally do with the letters you receive, if you ever were to receive any, that is?"

"They'd be thrown away. I've kept all of yours. They're at my house – I'll give them back to you. First we'll have to find you a job, right?"

Aurora was happy; you could really tell. She spent more time answering each question; she loved it when Guillermo asked her something, because each query opened up a new vista that she had never considered. Each question let her get to know another of his features, his registers. His face – tired; his eyebrows – thick; his nose; his lips . . . There was nothing out of the ordinary about him, yet something told her that he was in need of a little tender loving care. She wondered if every psychologist had the appropriate word for each moment, like Guillermo. But now it was her turn to ask a question.

"What do you mean by *we* will have to find a job?"

"Do you really think you're the only star in the sky? I've been a *hiring specialist* for five years now. That's the actual name of my position, and every day I ask myself if this is what I want to do. I look for drivers, checkout operators, administrative assistants . . ."

"Yes, you told me in your letter. And this isn't what you expected to be doing when you trained as a psychologist. What would you like to do?"

Now it was Guillermo's turn to feel slightly ashamed of his letter – the frank, open letter that he had sent to Aurora. They were on an equal fooling.

"What I like is observing human behaviour; I'd like nothing better than to work in the field of developmental psychology, perhaps as a camp counsellor . . . But I don't have time to look for a position, not even to think about it. My life is here. This is all I know; I'm here all day long, and when I'm out, I'm on the scooter, visiting the workplaces where we've placed people for our clients. I spend my weekends recuperating my energy for Monday. That's all."

His words came out with a leaden tone, weighed down by a burden that darkened his face and illuminated his eyes with a glassy light. Sorrow in rebellion. He hadn't been this frank with anyone for five long years, and Guillermo still had more to say.

"The good thing is that any wage they might offer me would seem magnificent in comparison with what I get paid here. Do you know how much I earn?"

"Not a clue."

"Less than the people I place. Less than a checkout boy, a warehouse clerk, a driver . . . And multiply that by all the hours I work. But more than that, it's that this job isn't my life's dream. I had the idea that here I'd be able to get inside people's personalities . . . But why kid myself? All I am is a middle man, up to my ears in work, finding people so that I can send them from here to there, and calling the people over there to tell 'em that the people from over here are on their way. And then, when they all sign the papers . . ."

"And have you found anything?"

"No! I'm not looking. It's expensive to live here, and I can't afford to take time off."

"Time to improve yourself," Aurora said.

"Jobs that pay must just be that, a way to make a living and nothing more." He sounded as though he were trying to convince himself. "Perhaps we ask too much of our workplaces. This isn't so bad, after all. We all know each other well, and *Talento* is a very respected firm in the field . . ." His voice had grown more formal.

He suddenly stood. Every time he got up like this, so abruptly, he startled Aurora, as he did now; so much energy put to waste, just in reaching for a box of files that was sitting by the door and grabbing a sheet of paper.

"Let's call that property management firm and ask about the position they had posted with us – want to?"

"OK," she said, uncertain.

There was a profound silence. Few things could make Aurora keep quiet, but now she was as closed-mouthed as when she took music classes in primary school and her teacher told the 20 boys and girls in the class to press their lips as tight as they could.

"Shhhhhh . . . Let's listen to what silence sounds like."

Silence also has its tonality. Aurora had learned that back then, and she had also discovered it since, in libraries. And now. Silence is no bother. Silence speaks.

All that could be heard was the dull sound of a finger dialling a phone number. A phone ringing. Again and again. Suddenly the personnel hiring specialist from the *Talento* Agency began speaking with the same conviction he always displayed towards his clients. Once more he had found a candidate who perfectly fitted their specifications. They could count on their caretaker's position to be filled by a fine professional woman, whom they could meet, with full references and the unanimous approval of *Talento*, and engage for a trial period at their earliest convenience.

But the sounds were muted once more, because the dialogue turned into a listening session. Perhaps some setback, or just a clarification about the position . . .

"Yes," Guillermo was saying without understanding why the answer was no.

In the course of the conversation, the psychologist found out that there was no position to be filled now, because the owners of the building had met the day before in extraordinary session and had agreed unanimously to sell the caretaker's flat in order to increase the communal budget. If their figures worked out correctly, everything seemed to point to their installing an entry-phone in the building.

"The situation changed just yesterday. I haven't had time to call you, and I didn't anticipate this turn of events. Pardon the bother, Guillermo," the building administrator said amiably.

Aurora had guessed what was happening from the psychologist's first silence. She was inured to setbacks. The really big ones made her stagger; anything else she reduced immediately to something minor. That was why she spent the rest of the interview looking calmly out of the window behind Guillermo's desk. Rain was hitting the aluminium frame and the glass window pane with a sound that was less distinct than distant hail falling on the lamp-posts in San Clemente de Quintás. It was much softer than the sound of rain falling into the gigantic aluminium tub that her grandmother used to leave out by the washing fountain and the clothes line.

"I like the rain," Aurora said, to save the psychologist the trouble of having to explain the setback as soon as he'd hung up the phone.

"Like when it rains in protest at the summer heat, or to soften the winter chill. Nature is alive; we aren't all alone." She improvised a new topic of conversation to lift the sadness that had fallen.

"There's no better way of finding out what people are like. Imagine a test: ten people, no umbrellas. It starts raining. What does each of them do? I think it's a perfect method," she said with a shade of enthusiasm. "It might even be useful for you psychologists. I think you can detect people's characters on a rainy day: you can see which ones always come prepared, which ones are spineless, which are dreamers, which are indifferent, which ones have all the time in the world and decide to spend it waiting in a doorway, which ones run, which are afraid to fall, which ones laugh, which frown, which go back inside their houses when they were all set to go out, which go out when they hadn't planned to go . . ."

"Aurora and her theories . . . And which of those are you?"

"I never carry an umbrella."

"But none of them have umbrellas."

"I look up at the sky. Sometimes the rain is full of colours."

"Must be the pollution."

"I feel lucky never to have studied." Aurora said, changing the subject.

"Don't lie."

"I didn't choose between the possibilities, so now I feel that I have all of them at once. The job opportunities nowadays do lots of damage, don't you think?"

"If you only knew the things we see here . . ." said the hiring specialist: a psychologist undergoing treatment, actually, for a colleague of his from medical school was treating him. This professional colleague offered him the usual: two kinds of pills, one to help him get to sleep, and another to feel able to combat the inexplicable sadness that overcame him during the few moments he managed to relax a little, such as now, as he talked to Aurora.

"'The Missing C.V. of Aurora Ortiz!'" said Guillermo, raising his voice as if he were citing the title of some grandiloquent film. He was trying to hide the crack in his voice. And he managed to do it.

He envied Aurora. Only when you have met with the deepest sorrow are you prepared never to be taken by it again. She was right: she was freer than anyone, and she could travel any path.

Several long minutes went by before his interviewee went home. Aurora was able to keep her slight disillusionment from taking on too much importance in the eyes of this man who was speaking to her and regaining the false calm of those suffering from depleted vitality. She even made the hiring specialist in him happy by letting him talk about the biological bases of behaviour and the thrilling pathways opened by smell, taste, dreams and food. His brown eyes recovered their sparkle when he told her about the times he had served as a summer counsellor in Navarra, in several camps organised for the children of sailors who had died at sea. That was when he was still in medical school. At the time, he also told her, he was 27 years old.

That was how old Roberto had been when he died, but Aurora didn't mention this. It had been three years, she thought once more. She kept quiet for the sake of the rain while she walked home, to the house that her husband had picked out with her – three years ago, also.

If he were holding her arm, under his umbrella, he would be telling her, as they walked home, about how tired he was after a tense morning of stressful work. She did let her husband protect her from the rain: it was an excuse for them to walk closer together, as they did that time – so long ago – that Roberto went to pick Aurora up at her Aunt Domi's shop. It had never rained so hard in San Clemente; seeing him walk in there with a modest black umbrella scarcely large enough to cover his shoulders made Aurora burst out laughing, and it also made it possible for them to rub cheeks together under the storm clouds on their way back to her house.

The umbrella was barely enough to keep their first kiss from being drowned in rain. That was why Aurora worshipped the water that falls from the sky.

That was why she never used umbrellas again.

CHAPTER XXI

Madrid
15 November 2000

Dear Clemente,

I am a lucky person. I'm writing again on a borrowed computer, the one that belongs to my neighbour, Fany. The other day, when she was off work for the holiday, we had a long breakfast together. It had been ages since we had seen each other. She still doesn't want to have her computer back, which I think is a shame, because she writes so well. She says that all she needs is a pencil and a sheet of paper, but her professional life as a checkout operator wears her out; I found her very low in energy, to tell the truth.

I'm fine. Since I've been back, I've had several interviews with the agency that I've mentioned to you in the past. I'm all confused, Clemente. People are dying to get jobs, but when they're working at their jobs, they start dying all over again, because they do so much damage to their restless curiosity that they hardly feel their final rest approaching.

Apart from the mortgage on the flat, I hardly have any expenses, and I have a widow's pension that allows me to face life without having to despair – that's what the woman psychologist who interviewed me must have reckoned when

I told her that I wanted to be the caretaker of a building, and she called me a girl with a whim. In fact, I think that's what she actually did call me. How can a supposed expert in investigating the inner mind of the person she's interviewing be so mistaken?

When Roberto was studying for his entrance examination for Renfe, we lived from the hours I spent cleaning houses, far from my neighbourhood. I didn't mention this in the interview, but it was the second job I've had in my life. Hours spent with dirty plates and dusty corners, stained sheets and unironed shirts.

Believe me, I made some good friends, even among important people with top positions in big firms. They'd often end up inviting me to have coffee, and we'd discuss the news of the week and what we had read that month. We'd exchange books; once I even went so far as to lend one of my library books to the president of a British bank for five days. I don't know where he found the time – everybody in that house was always so busy – but he finished it before it was due back. He liked it as much as I had, and he was so grateful to me for lending it to him that it made me wonder how someone who had so much money that he could buy whole collections of books and display them in massive bookcases of Spanish walnut could still appreciate a simple book from a municipal library. He told me that the most valuable things in life are free; at the time I thought that only people who have a good salary coming in at the end of the month think that way. Now I realise I was wrong. When he returned the book to me, we sat talking in the living room for as many hours as I had spent altogether in cleaning the bathrooms, vacuuming, ironing and cooking.

"Aurora, let me know if there's anything you need," he told me one day. Maybe I'll call on them this Christmas.

I liked working. Any job was fine, because Roberto was

waiting for me at home. After he was hired to work at the North Madrid train station, I quit cleaning houses and started working with a group of women from Ecuador without work permits while I explored the best way to get back to books. Then came the big shock, one fine day.

Now I need to work, but I don't have anybody waiting for me at home; that's why I thought it would be a good idea for me to leave home. Change my surroundings, cross the threshold to another house. Believe me, Clemente, often when I'm walking down the street, I stop in front of the buildings that have caretakers' offices. I bury my head inside them like an ostrich.

It isn't easy to become a caretaker. In the smaller buildings, the tendency is to replace caretakers with entry-phones; in the big ones, the style now is to hire a concierge or even a security guard. The advantage of having a concierge, I've been told, is that, although they earn higher wages than caretakers would, they still reduce the overall costs to the owners, since they don't live in the building.

Guillermo, the hiring specialist at the agency, has supplied me with information about these topics just in case a new opportunity presents itself. The other day, he even gave me a copy of the *Labour Agreement for Employees of Town Properties*. My eyes were sparkling with joy when I saw my fondest dreams reflected in that document: "A *caretaker* is a person who is given a room to live in as his home in the building, and who enjoys a labour contract." Then it spoke about the caretaker's duties, and they all pleased me – cleaning, maintenance, and upkeep of the entranceway, caretaker's office, stairs, and other common areas; turning on and off and maintaining the heating system, the hot water, the lifts, and the service lifts. Keeping watch on vacant flats, and accompanying prospective tenants who want to see them; opening and closing the front gate; controlling the lights in common areas; removing the rubbish. I found out that there are even prizes and fines, depending on the caretaker's behaviour. Did you know that one of the prizes is to pay for courses to raise the caretaker's cultural awareness, or to offer instructional trips?

Forgive me for spending this whole letter talking about work. I've been asked so many questions over the past few days that I can only see myself in this dimension . . . This is turning out to be my latest routine.

I'm fine. I have an urge to go back and take walks along the river, talk with you, and see everybody else. If I had email, this letter would get to you before I even turned off the computer, but there's no need to be in such a rush. When I go out to help the Ecuadorians, I'll pass by the letter box on the corner.

A week from now I'll be heading back to that big house with its wide door and no caretaker. I long to see the chestnut trees, see the whole orchard, spend my hours on the balcony. And rest. More than anything, I want to think. I've met several people lately who never think, they just decide.

They decide, therefore, they are.

. . . It just occurs to me: on the last day of the year, we could organise a huge bonfire in the village. Mention it to my Aunt Domi; my head is swarming with hopes and dreams. Each time you jump over the bonfire, one dream will come true in the coming millennium. Easy as that, don't you think?

My new year is still on its way. And the new century. We can't be impassive, no . . . But for now, calm.

I trust you've read *aurora.doc*. At the time, I told you goodbye; now, I'm saying see you soon. Merry Christmas. I'll bring carrot pastries – I think that's a common custom in Germany, isn't it, Advent pastries? You would know better . . . I've bought a pastry mix from a Swedish grocery. It's easier that way.

My flat looks completely different. I can't believe how empty it is. The people who relate minimalism with the turn of the century are going to turn out to be right, after all; the less you have, in any case, the less strain it is on your eyes.

There's going to be a Christmas jumble sale in the neighbourhood, and I've donated several pieces of furniture and lots of small items. Now I realise that the walls need painting – you can see where things used to be. I've bought several colours to mix, but that will have to wait until I get back from San Clemente. I want to invent a colour, a colour that no one else has invented. Is that possible? It'll have to be, because I already have the name for it. It's been decided: the colour is called rain.

*

"A new colour . . ." Clemente tore his eyes from the letter and stirred the embers in the wood stove.

There were just a few more lines to read. The words of farewell. But those lines remained unread, because a light entered through the window of the old school building. Perhaps it was the mixture of the smoke from the kitchen stove and the rain that produced a strange effect outside. If it weren't for the condensation on the window pane, which of course can trick your eyes sometimes, you would have sworn that an aurora borealis had suddenly left a trail reflected in the river . . .

And it flew away, towards the north, at full speed.

ACKNOWLEDGEMENTS

Thanks to Protestant ministers Klaus Looft and Samuel Pimentel, and to psychologist Guillermo Madroñal, with whom I worked for a valuable fictitious period in a temporary recruitment agency. My thanks to all three for generously answering so many basic questions during the first steps of this novel's conception, when I devoted myself to talking and talking without writing a word. Thanks to Professor Francisco de Moxó y Montoliu for sharing his wisdom, with Bach as a pretext, in the Music School of the University of San Pablo, CEU, in Madrid. To Francisco J. Solana Bajo, for the poetry he gave me as a gift, and which belongs to him, though it now forms part of this novel . . .

Thanks to Ángeles Mastretta for her tremendous generosity. I also thank those friends who became my first readers for their valuable comments, especially Julio Llamazares for his ready embrace. To the great reader Mercedes Milá for being as overjoyed as I was to find out that Aurora Ortiz and her C.V. would finally be leaving my house.

I would like to give a quiet shout of thanks to the energising silence of the library, and to my parents, who led me there with the same assurance that they later showed in taking me to ride the bumper cars. Thanks, of course, to Elizabeth Atkins, my agent, and to Rosa Ruocco, my editor, for letting me begin.